HARLEQUIN®
Presents~

Summer's here, and to get you in the mood we've got some sizzling reads for you this month!

So relax and enjoy…a scandalous proposal in *Bought for Revenge, Bedded for Pleasure* by Emma Darcy; a virgin bride in *Virgin: Wedded at the Italian's Convenience* by Diana Hamilton; a billionaire's bargain in *The Billionaire's Blackmailed Bride* by Jacqueline Baird; a sexy Spaniard in *Spanish Billionaire, Innocent Wife* by Kate Walker; and an Italian's marriage ultimatum in *The Salvatore Marriage Deal* by Natalie Rivers. And be sure to read *The Greek Tycoon's Baby Bargain*, the first book in Sharon Kendrick's brilliant new duet, GREEK BILLIONAIRES' BRIDES.

Plus, two new authors bring you their dazzling debuts—Natalie Anderson with *His Mistress by Arrangement*, and Anne Oliver with *Marriage at the Millionaire's Command*. Don't miss out!

We'd love to hear what you think about Presents. E-mail us at Presents@hmb.co.uk or join in the discussions at www.iheartpresents.com and www.sensationalromance.blogspot.com, where you'll also find more information about books and authors!

Private jets. Luxury cars. Exclusive five-star hotels. Designer outfits for every occasion and an entourage of staff to see to your every whim....

In this brand-new collection, ordinary women step into the world of the super-rich and are

TAKEN BY THE
MILLIONAIRE

He'll have her—but at what price?

Anne Oliver

MARRIAGE AT THE MILLIONAIRE'S COMMAND

TAKEN BY THE
MILLIONAIRE

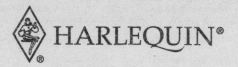

HARLEQUIN®

TORONTO • NEW YORK • LONDON
AMSTERDAM • PARIS • SYDNEY • HAMBURG
STOCKHOLM • ATHENS • TOKYO • MILAN • MADRID
PRAGUE • WARSAW • BUDAPEST • AUCKLAND

ISBN-13: 978-0-373-12738-2
ISBN-10:   0-373-12738-3

MARRIAGE AT THE MILLIONAIRE'S COMMAND

First North American Publication 2008.

Previously published in the U.K. under the title
ONE NIGHT BEFORE MARRIAGE.

All about the author...
Anne Oliver

When not teaching or writing, **ANNE OLIVER** loves nothing more than escaping into a book. She keeps a box of tissues handy—her favorite stories are intense, passionate, against-all-odds romances. Eight years ago she began creating her own characters in paranormal and time-travel adventures, before turning to contemporary romance. Other interests include quilting, astronomy, all things Scottish and eating anything she doesn't have to cook. Sharing her characters' journeys with readers all over the world is a privilege…and a dream come true. Anne lives in Adelaide, South Australia, and has two adult children. Visit her Web site at www.anne-oliver.com. She loves to hear from readers. E-mail her at anne@anne-oliver.com.

Marriage at the Millionaire's Command was written during a period of personal upheaval, only to come second in the Romance Writers of New Zealand's 2004 Clendon Award for a full novel!

This one's for you, Mum!

Also, thanks to my great critique team and to editors Kimberley Young and Meg Sleightholme for their valuable insight and revision suggestions to the original manuscript.

CHAPTER ONE

THE scent of her grandmother's perfume was the first sign. The prickle at her nape was the second. While Gran's scent was benign and loving and familiar, the second sign sent a shiver down her spine.

Carissa Grace never ignored signs.

Anxious, she scanned the stream of cars outside Sydney's Cove Hotel. Her stepsister Melanie had insisted on picking her up since Carissa's gig at the piano bar had finished after midnight tonight. That had been twenty minutes ago.

Hurry up, Mel. Something's—

The screech of brakes sheared through the balmy night, an agony of metal on metal over the mellow sound of sax drifting from a nearby nightclub. As the dented Holden mounted the kerb, its headlights loomed like silver lasers before her, terrifyingly stark against the subtle orange glow of the city night.

For a stunned second Carissa couldn't move. She was one with the crowd as it held its collective breath, movement halted, time suspended, minds frozen.

An instant later the car was gone, leaving only the acrid smell of exhaust fumes and hot bitumen.

'Anyone hurt?' a male voice demanded in a deep timbre that rippled down Carissa's spine like an arpeggio. In the awed hush that followed, a man emerged from the knot of people huddled against the hotel's sparkling lobby windows.

Tall, broad-shouldered. Awesome. He looked as dangerous as the chaos around him, from the heavily shadowed jaw and unkempt brown hair that curled over his neck to the faded black jeans and T-shirt. Not the kind of man she'd have expected to get involved in anything but trouble. Every 'bad boy' fantasy Carissa had ever had vibrated into shocking—and inappropriate—awareness.

'Someone call an ambulance.' His order snapped with authority.

Then she saw the form sprawled on the concrete. In two strides he was there, crouching over the slumped figure, speaking low. It was an old woman, Carissa realised, the bag lady she'd seen scrounging through the bin only moments ago. Despite the heat, she was covered from neck to ankle in a filthy coat. Her limbs flailed as she struggled up.

With no hesitation the man scooped a hand beneath her head, holding her against his thigh, murmuring soothing noises against her ear.

Carissa pulled herself together and hurried to rescue the woman's over-stuffed garbage bag nearby. Ignoring the crowd, which was curious but unwilling to get involved, Carissa set the bag down and crouched beside them. 'Here you go.'

The woman shot her an accusing glare as she grabbed the plastic.

'Is she okay?' Carissa asked.

'I reckon so,' he said, taking the woman's dirt-smudged fingers in his own large hand. 'But I'll get her checked out to be sure.' Preoccupied with his patient, he didn't look at Carissa.

Mingled with the odour of unwashed woman, she detected the distinct smell of male. A purely feminine appreciation sharpened her senses. It had been a long time since she'd smelled earthy masculine sweat. Alasdair always smelled of fancy French cologne. Nor could she imagine her fiancé handling this situation with such calm confidence.

The man sat the woman upright and stroked her back through

the coat. His forearm twisted, drawing Carissa's attention to the gleaming silver of an expensive watch on his wrist. A disconcerting tingle spread through her limbs as she watched the muscles bunch and flex beneath his tanned skin. 'Do you think you can—?' A car's horn drowned the rest of his words to the old woman.

Carissa glanced at the street. Her ride. She raised a hand to Melanie as she backed away. Clearly he had everything under control and didn't need her assistance.

'Sorry I'm late,' Mel said as Carissa climbed in. 'Emergency was a war zone tonight. What's going on?' She honked her horn again and pulled into the traffic.

'We've had something of our own war zone.' Carissa's heart was still pounding with the drama. 'It's all under control now.' Thanks to the hero of the day.

Her gaze remained glued to the man as he ushered the bag lady towards the Cove's gleaming entrance. She could see the powerful square shape of his shoulders and his black T-shirt taut over one thick bicep.

A wildly sexy, *dangerous* man. He looked as if he'd just stepped out of one of her forbidden erotic dreams. The ones she'd been having with disturbingly increasing regularity of late.

She let out a sigh. She'd not seen Alasdair in a year, which made any man with half the rugged sex appeal of that stranger dangerous.

Not that she hadn't been more than willing to wait while Alasdair finished his PhD in France. But the promised twelve weeks had stretched into twelve long months.

She took one last look at temptation before turning to the red rear lights of the cars in front. A girl could only wait so long before that temptation reached out to tickle her fancy.

She shook away the delicious little shiver at the thought of the stranger's long, thick fingers reaching out to tickle *her* fancy... And bit back a moan. It was sexual frustration, that was all.

In seven days Alasdair would be home, and her bed was

already turned down in anticipation. There'd be no more of that waiting he'd told her was the 'right thing' to do. Her already sensitised body hummed at the thought. Everything would be fine when Alasdair came back.

'Alasdair's not coming back.'

With the single handwritten page in her fist, Carissa sat down on the back step beside Melanie. The numbness had worn off enough to trust herself to talk about it. Rationally. Calmly. Maybe.

Mel's eyes widened. 'Oh, Carrie.' She set her iced tea on the verandah and reached for Carissa's hand. 'I'm so sorry,' she said quietly. 'You two have been together, what, seven years? What happened?'

'He's met someone else. I should've expected it with him studying overseas and all those chic mademoiselle research assistants.' She closed her eyes. 'But I *didn't* expect him to tell me his new love's name is *Pierre.*'

'Oh. God.' Melanie let out a slow breath. 'I don't know what to say.' She twined their fingers together. 'Are you okay?'

'I will be.' Carissa squeezed their hands briefly, then stood. A restless energy she didn't know what to do with was coursing through her body. 'I trusted him; I waited for him. Even though I wasn't sure any more that he was the One, I waited, at least until I saw him again. I must be the world's most naïve fool.'

'No. It's not your fault he's a two-timing creep—in the worst way. You sure you're okay?'

'Fine.' Enclosing that energy into a tight fist, she crumpled the paper and squinted against the glare of the parched backyard. The hot summer wind kicked up, rattling the loose drainpipe she hadn't gotten around to fixing yet.

'It's been so long, I'm used to it. My life will go on as usual. I've got my own place, such as it is.' She frowned at the sagging porch trim. Her grandparents' old home needed major repairs. 'And a job.'

'You've still got me,' Mel said quietly.

'I know.' She met Mel's eyes with shared affection before turning away. 'Want to know a secret, Mel? I've still got my well-past-its-use-by-date virginity.'

'You mean you and Alasdair never...? Oh...'

Carissa paced up the verandah and back. 'Now I know why Alasdair was so noble and self-sacrificing. Every time I came on to him he said I'd thank him for making me wait.'

'So...days before your twenty-sixth birthday, you're still a virgin?' Melanie blew out a breath. 'Wow.'

'At this rate, on my fifty-sixth birthday, I'll be taking out a full-page ad.'

The urge to lash out rose up like a black wave. She needed to channel the energy productively. Some serious piano-pounding. Something dark and passionate. Bach, she decided. The flyscreen door squeaked on rusty hinges as she swung it open.

Melanie followed. 'Do you really want your life to go on as usual? No man, no sex, no fun?'

Carissa's hand paused on the door. *Don't answer that.*

'You need a fling, Carrie, a one-night stand.'

The suggestion was outrageous. And at this point Carissa felt almost reckless enough to consider it. 'You know, Mel, I just might take your advice.' She tossed the balled paper in the bin on her way.

'Don't rush it, though,' Mel warned as if she'd gone cold on the idea already. 'You want your piano tuned, you don't call a plumber.'

'So what's wrong with a plumber if he's got the right equipment?' Carissa couldn't help smiling at Mel's frown. She slung an arm around the one person she could always count on to look out for her. 'I'll be careful.'

The usual Saturday evening crowd buzzed in the Cove Hotel's piano bar. Carissa's eyes roamed the faces while she played her selection of dreamy Chopin nocturnes. She noted the few regulars, but most were anonymous tourists with a couple of hours to kill before heading off to Sydney's nightclubs.

So much for finding a man. Working six evenings a week seriously impinged on one's social life. She hadn't had a social life in so long, she wasn't sure she was ready for centre stage in the dating scene just yet.

She saw him the moment he entered the room.

He filled the doorway, all six-feet-four-if-he-was-an-inch of him. Her fingers faltered as she drank in the rock-solid body crammed into faded denim and black T-shirt.

Her mouth watered. God help her, if she could choose, she wanted that body, naked and next to hers. It was the kind of body that made women forget all about sexual equality—there was absolutely nothing *equal* about it.

Her fingers automatically drifted into *Moonlight Sonata* as her eyes followed him to the bar. She watched him order a beer, then move to a table near the window where the last rays of sunset turned the water beyond to liquid fire and the white tablecloths crimson, and glittered on his fancy silver watch.

Oh. My. God. It was the guy she'd seen last night. Her pulse rate zipped straight off her personal Richter Scale. He'd shaved.

But he was still dangerous.

She shifted on her stool for a better view of yesterday's hero. The evening glow accentuated the angular contours of a tanned face on the wrong side of pretty-boy handsome and a strong, shadowed jaw. Mid-thirties, give or take. His teak-coloured hair, although shorter, was still somewhat dishevelled, as if he'd run his fingers through it, prompting images of lazy lust-filled afternoons on black silk sheets.

She should be so lucky.

But he had the most soulful eyes she'd ever seen. She reached for her mineral water, checked her watch and sighed. Two hours and ten minutes till she finished for the night—but he'd be gone by then.

* * *

Ben Jamieson flicked an eye over the pianist, then returned for a longer, in-depth perusal. And decided his evening had just taken a turn for the better. Why spend it alone dwelling on his own personal anguish when the distraction he needed was right here?

Rave would tell him to go for it— he could almost see his mate grin and raise a glass in salute to women everywhere. For tonight at least he could appreciate the soothing harbour view while he watched those clever—and ringless—fingers on the keys.

Kicking back, he took a large gulp of beer and studied her. The way those fingers tickled the ivories, he imagined they could do a pretty good job on a man.

So classical wasn't his thing. The classic lines of the pianist more than made up for it. That full-length slinky sapphire number she'd poured herself into begged to be taken off. Slowly, an inch at a time. You didn't hurry over a body like that.

Tall, he noted, but not too tall. Like a long, slim candle. He'd bet she'd burn with a cool blue flame, and damned if he didn't want to singe his fingers. And that hair—a loose twist of sunshine at the crown of her head, held by a sequinned clasp. There was something about upswept hair that made his fingers itch. That smooth, exposed nape, and all that silk tumbling into his hands.

It was shaping up to be an interesting evening after all.

As Carissa launched into another bracket of light classics she couldn't resist another peek. He didn't look the classical type. His music preferences didn't bother her. His head turned as if he'd felt her watching him, and their gazes collided over the raised lid of the baby grand. Instant heat flooded her body.

She dragged her eyes away, fumbled with the keys again and swore softly. She'd played the cocktail bar Friday and Saturday nights for two years and not missed a note. With her brain threatening meltdown, she reached for her sheet music and refused to look his way again.

Concentrate on the important issues, she reminded herself. Such as not losing this gig and how she was going to pay the land-tax bill. Her Monday to Thursday job at the suburban café paid half what she made here. Even the extra money a lodger would bring in would only skim the top of the pile, and if she didn't get someone pronto she'd have to advertise beyond the staff cafeteria; something she didn't want to do. Always risky for a woman living alone.

She'd always been able to put distractions aside when she played. Not tonight. Tonight she couldn't raise the shield that shut out the rest of the world. She was all too aware of the clink of glass and ice and money, conversation, the light outside as it changed from dusk to dark.

And him.

At ten-thirty Carissa closed the piano, shuffled her music into a neat pile and slipped it into its folder.

'Can I buy you a drink?' The deep liquid voice with its hint of gravel made her jump.

The scent of aftershave and beer hit her as she turned, her habit of a cool smile and polite refusal already on her lips, but the words died in her throat.

Something like panic leapt up and grabbed her by the throat, then worked down to her stomach, squeezing the air out of her lungs on its way. 'Sorry, management doesn't permit employees to socialise with guests.'

Refusing—was she nuts? Taking a deep breath, the new, unattached Carissa smiled. 'Leastways, not in the hotel.'

He grinned. 'A walk, then, and a drink by the waterfront. The name's Ben Jamieson.' One corner of his mouth lifted crookedly, revealing the most kissable dimple in his right cheek. Up close she saw that his eyes were bright jungle-green and sparking with interest.

She clutched her folder to her chest to hide the sudden tremble in her hands. 'I've a train and a bus to catch, and I don't like to leave it too late.'

'I'll pay your cab fare home.'

'Oh…I…'

'Walk with me. It's a pleasant evening and we'll only go as far as you want.'

Those erotic images popped into her head again, but if he'd intended it as a double entendre he was astute enough to show no sign.

She smiled as she pushed in the piano stool. 'It's the best offer I've had all night.' The best in years, in fact, and the mind-set was still taking some adjustment.

'Why don't you start by telling me your name?'

'Carissa.' She kept her eyes on his, aware of his body heat, his fresh soap smell, his masculinity. *Dangerous,* she warned herself. 'Just Carissa.'

He smiled again, and everything inside her melted a few more degrees. 'So, Just Carissa, do you have a bag or something?'

'In the staff locker room. I'll change and meet—'

'No.' His eyes didn't leave hers, but their green fire scorched all the way to her toes. 'Do me a favour—don't.'

She cleared her throat. 'Okay… But I need my bag.'

He accompanied her past the press of bodies at the bar, and across the foyer, checked his messages—ah, he was a residential guest—while she headed for the locker room.

Her brain was a whirl; her insides were doing a quick shuffle. To waltz off with a complete stranger—she'd never done anything so impulsive or so reckless.

'Why don't we combine the two and walk to the station?' she suggested as they walked out into Sydney's tropical summer evening.

Streetlights attracted bugs, which hummed in a seething ball around the globes. A languid breeze drifted off the water.

He glanced at her. 'Why? Is someone expecting you?'

If she was going to back out, now was the time. But he was on a first name basis with the concierge, had a room there, and people had seen them leave together. 'There's no one.'

'I don't like the idea of a woman catching a train alone at this time of night. Then a bus, for heaven's sake. Do you always travel by public transport?'

'Since I sold the car.'

His hand touched the small of her back as he ushered her to a table at an open-air café. Just a brush of fingertips on the silk of her dress, but the thrill curled her toes inside her four-inch stilettos.

'What would you like?'

You. 'Mineral water over ice, thank you.' She sagged onto the plastic chair he pulled out for her and slipped her bag onto the ground beside her feet. She didn't need anything stronger to have that dizzy, tipsy rush.

He paid at the counter, handed her a glass and lowered himself into the chair opposite with a bottle of beer. 'Here's looking at you.'

The way he said that had shivers chasing over her skin. To distract him from her nipples that suddenly puckered painfully into tight little buds against her dress she asked, 'You like music?' He didn't reply and a shadow crossed his eyes. She watched his fist tighten infinitesimally around the neck of his bottle. 'Okay, you don't like classical and you're too polite to say so.'

'Doesn't matter what it is when it's played with heart and soul by a woman whose…what colour would you say your eyes are?'

She blinked, glass poised halfway to her lips. 'Blue.'

'Blue.' He rubbed a hand over his jaw, a distinctively masculine sound, as he watched her. 'I'd say ultramarine. Deep and mysterious. Which begs a question: what do you do when you're not at the keyboard, Just Carissa?'

'Waitressing and piano take up six days a week. I don't have time for much else.'

It amazed her that she could sit here and make reasonable conversation with this man when all she could think of was what he'd look like with every inch of golden skin bared for her pleasure, every working part primed to— *Stop right there*. She mentally slapped herself and asked, 'What about you?'

He glanced at the water, avoiding her gaze. 'I have a few business interests.'

She eyed him over her glass. 'When you're not being a hero.'

'I beg your pardon?'

'Last night. I was outside the Cove, I saw you.'

He took a deep gulp of beer. The shadows were back in his eyes. 'I'm no hero.'

'Wrong. I was there. You risked yourself for others, stopped to help an old lady most people would avoid.'

'No big deal. And it was hardly a risk; the car was gone. Those stupid kids…' He shook his head. 'We'll all end up in the sewer one day.'

'You're not an optimist, then. You don't believe good outweighs bad? That everything happens for a reason?'

He seemed to remember something sad because his mouth thinned even more, and he smiled without humour. 'I'm more of a realist. Realists are rarely disappointed.'

He had a point there. A realist would have expected Alasdair to walk. Good-looking guys, whatever their gender preference, didn't hang around for long. 'What about your family?' *Is there a fiancée waiting to be jilted somewhere?*

'I grew up in Melbourne. Never married, never tempted. Lived in the outback, came to the city a few years ago.'

'Your parents?'

'Mum's in Melbourne. My father's dead.'

End of story. Chewing her lip, Carissa watched him toss back the contents of his bottle. His father's death must have hit him hard and he didn't want to talk about it. 'Are you staying at the Cove long?'

'Not sure yet.'

She saw the residual tension in his hand as he set the empty bottle on the table with a clunk. The man had problems. Did she want to get involved? But she remembered last night. He was one of the good guys. Besides, she wasn't getting *involved* involved.

'Come on,' he said, slowly reverting to the flirtatious man she'd started out with. 'It'll be cooler by the water.'

They left the glare of lights and wandered to where the air was shadowed and filled with the scent of sea and summer. Carissa took off her shoes and lifted her face to the faint breeze. 'I've worked at the Cove for two years and never walked here.'

'A night for firsts.'

She almost smiled. He didn't know the half of it.

He stopped and looked down at her. 'Do you know what I was thinking about while I was watching you play?'

'What?' The word spilled out on a husky, almost breathless exhalation.

He lowered his mouth till it was a sigh away from hers. 'This.' He skimmed her lips with his own, a tantalising hint. 'Touching you. Tasting you.'

Oh, yes, she thought, her mouth tingling with the promise. *Me too.*

He tangled calloused fingers with hers, watching her. Still watching her, he deliberately pressed his body against hers. One body part in particular. One very thick, very hard, very insistent body part.

She didn't step back. He was big, he was male, and, unlike her ex-fiancé, he wanted her. He lowered his lips again, and, dropping her shoes, she leaned into him, her bag skimming her hip as she wound her arms around his neck.

Her mind shut down. Her senses went into overdrive. The flavour of his mouth, beer and something salty, the textures of tongue and teeth as he deepened the kiss, his roughened fingertips skimming her arms.

After the first flutter of nerves she relaxed and acquainted herself with the new and exciting sensation of male arousal against her belly. So far, so good, but how would it feel horizontally? With no clothes on?

She wanted to know how it felt to have a man's weight on her, to have him pumping all that heat and strength inside her. She wanted to know whether fantasy lived up to reality. And she wanted *this* man to be the one to show her.

She'd never have to see him again. If she didn't ask more personal questions, didn't get to know him, she could walk away, no emotional ties, the way men did. Her birthday present to herself. She hadn't taken anything for herself in a long time. And Melanie would definitely approve.

He pulled back, hands on her elbows, his eyes dark with lusty impatience. 'What do you want to do about this?'

A ball of heat lodged in her gut, her knees went weak, her pulse hammered. Keeping her eyes on his, she reached up, trailed unsteady hands down the unfamiliar contours of his neck.

Sex with a stranger. Through his T-shirt she rubbed over his tight little nipples with her thumbs before moving over the plane of chest and stomach to the fabric's hem. She crept her fingers underneath and found hot, hard flesh. Then she hooked her hands in the waistband of his jeans. And tugged.

His stomach muscles tensed against her knuckles. His breath jerked in. He'd think her easy and experienced. She stifled an almost hysterical laugh.

'Carissa, I can put you in a cab now, or we can continue this in my room. The decision's yours.' Restless hips shifted against her fingers. 'But make it quick.'

Something hot and dangerous shot through her body like a flame-tipped arrow. She only had to say, and she could be in his room. In his bed.

In the Cove Hotel.

She let out a frustrated breath. 'Employees aren't permitted in guests' rooms.'

'Is that a "no" or a problem?'

'A…problem?' She shrugged. 'Rules are rules.'

His eyes crinkled at the corners as he watched her. He smiled that crooked smile as he took her hands from his jeans, rubbed a thumb over her knuckles. 'So we'll break a few rules.'

CHAPTER TWO

THEY separated before they reached the door and met again at the elevator. Shocked, Carissa watched as Ben keyed his card. 'The penthouse?'

'I like space and a room with a view.'

Seconds later the elevator doors whooshed open. She stepped into the room and stared. Low lighting didn't dim the view of Sydney's coat-hanger bridge, the Opera House like luminous swans on the harbour. The room was black on white. Silver glinted, marble shone. The whole scene screamed money. 'Wow.'

He moved to the full-length glass door, slid it open. Sheer curtains billowed in on the sultry breeze. 'One of the best views in the world,' he said.

She hadn't come for the view. She hadn't even come for romance.

She'd come for sex.

And the man of the moment lounged against the balcony with wind in his hair, an intriguing blend of casual and remote as he stared over the water. Her first lover, a man she didn't know.

The jolt of realisation must have shown on her face because when he finally looked at her, the expression warmed. 'Relax and come here.'

She swallowed and stayed where she was. 'I want you to

know, I'm not in the habit— I mean…this isn't…' Now she was babbling and way out of her depth.

'I like you pink and flustered. An interesting contrast to that cool, classical beauty at the piano.'

Shifting into defence mode, she lifted her chin. 'I am not flustered.' But she did relax when she saw the glint of humour in his eyes as he came towards her.

'Okay, then…' He trailed fingers of fire up the side of her neck and into her hair under her clasp at the back of her head. 'Sophisticated *naïveté.*'

A buzzer dinged. Her eyes whipped to the elevator door.

'Hey.' He squeezed her nape. 'I told you to relax. Admire the view a moment.'

She turned away and waited out the brief exchange and the sound of the doors sliding shut before turning back.

'Happy Valentine's Day. Red roses for a blue lady.' He held out the dozen perfect long-stemmed buds.

Oh, my. Something inside her sparkled, like a snowflake under the first rays of spring sunshine. No one had ever given her flowers. 'They're beautiful, thank you.' She buried her nose in their rich velvety fragrance. 'But Valentine's Day was yesterday.'

'Somewhere in the world it still is.'

'How did you manage these? It's after midnight.'

'The gift shop's always open for the right people.'

What did he mean by that? Who *was* Ben Jamieson? Someone important? Obviously someone with money to burn.

Still, something about being here with him, surrounded by the fragrance of summer roses, made her want to weep. She'd never think of Valentine's Day again without remembering Ben Jamieson. He'd reached deep inside her and found something she'd been determined to keep buried. Need. A need for more than simple lust.

But with that need came vulnerability. *Don't get emotionally involved. You're walking away tonight; you'll never see him again.* 'You shouldn't have,' she said, caressing a bud.

'Why not?' He tipped her chin up. 'You in that blue dress makes me wish I could whisk you away to the top of the Sydney Tower. Just us and the stars.'

Clasping her hand, he led her to the balcony where said tower shone like a golden lollipop. Lights shimmered on black water. Somewhere below music drifted, the breeze sighed.

This wasn't supposed to happen. With gentle persuasion he was changing something simple into something romantic and complicated.

He took the roses, laid them on the smoked-glass table and cupped her face before lowering his lips.

Again his mouth was firm yet soft, and moved over hers in a slow, sensuous kiss that had her mind blotting out all thoughts but the mindless pleasure of it. His hands moved to her shoulders, kneading away the growing tension.

Her world was suddenly intense, alive and filled with colour and movement. She heard the muted noise of traffic and a distant ferry's horn as he pulled her closer. The sensation of falling, spinning, had her clutching at his chest, sleek muscle over bone.

'Come with me.' Twining their fingers together, he walked her through an arch to the adjoining room.

The bedroom was as impressive as the rest of the suite. A single black-shaded lamp threw out a muted, seductive glow in one corner. The king-size bed had been turned down for the night and her heart leapt at its intimate invitation.

Skilled fingers slipped inside the back of her dress and down. The zipper slid open with a whisper, the hooks of her bra loosened. Smoothing his hands over her shoulders, he skimmed down her arms until her dress and bra fell to the floor and she stood only in high-cut sapphire panties, lace-topped thigh-high blue stockings and spiky-heeled shoes.

His eyes darkened and he stepped back. 'Leave them on,' he said as her fingers moved to her thighs. 'I want to look.'

Goosebumps chased over her body; her nipples puckered and

throbbed. The whole thing was surreal; she felt like a model in a men's magazine.

He blew out a long breath, arms crossed over his chest. 'You're a living fantasy. Now take off the panties—slowly. Very slowly.'

With an excitement she'd never felt, she hooked her fingers in the skinny blue straps and slid them down her thighs. She could see the sweat beading his brow as he shifted his stance, drawing her attention away from his face to the straining and impressive bulge in his jeans. Oh, God.

He gestured to the discarded undies. 'Put them on the bed.'

Why? Then she felt his eyes consume her body as she bent down to obey his request and knew the answer.

'Now release your hair. With both hands.'

Her breasts lifted with the movement, swollen and heavy. She let out an uneven breath as she tossed the clasp on the floor and separated the thick strands. He'd barely touched her and she was glowing.

'Anticipation's half the fun,' he murmured. But he sure didn't smile as if he was having fun. A muscle in his jaw clenched; his mouth hardened.

Her cheeks were on fire, and, yes, anticipation—every pulse point hammered with it. She focused on his gaze and told him with her eyes.

But he didn't reach for her. With a swift tug, he rid himself of his T-shirt, tossed it on the floor beside her dress. His eyes burned. 'Touch me.'

She swallowed over a healthy dose of nerves. Clothed, no problem, but alone with a semi-naked man and knowing he was going to get a lot more naked any minute… What if he wanted her to do…something she didn't know how to do?

Get a grip, he's only asked you to touch him. So far. Tentative, she touched the dark hair sprinkled over that massive chest, felt the texture against the warm, hard skin beneath. She trailed her fingers lower, following the line of hair to his navel and below, where his jeans rode low on his hips...

Taking her hand, he pressed it against his thick, throbbing erection and squeezed. Heat burned through his jeans; his body jerked. Very soon, that heat, that hardness was going to be inside her. The last thing she needed was a pregnancy. She gazed up into his eyes again. 'You do have protection. Don't you?'

'It's okay, Carissa. I won't let anything happen to you. Trust me.' Then with a growl he tumbled her backwards onto the bed. One shoe fell to the floor. A flick of his wrist and his jeans snapped open. He pushed them off his hips, down his legs with his boxers and a hard, hairy thigh nudged between her legs.

The contrasts were stunning. His heat, the angles and planes of his masculine body, the coolness of the crisp cotton sheet, the sultry air against her dewy skin.

Soft light played over bronzed flesh and hard-packed muscle and his, oh...his restless hands as they slid across her belly and up over her breasts. He sifted his fingers through her hair with a murmur of masculine appreciation.

Lowering his head, he closed his mouth over one nipple, then the other. She felt the tug all the way to the soles of her curled feet. She arched her back on a moan as sensation layered over sensation.

The stockings were last to go. He took his slow sweet time, his fingers brushing aside the nylon, laying a sensuous trail of kisses behind until there wasn't a square inch of skin that wasn't tingling. Except where she wanted him most.

At last, when she didn't think she could stand it any longer, he parted her thighs with his hand and slid a finger over moist flesh that had never been touched. She went weak, moaned again. She'd never dreamed it could feel this...*good*.

He was familiar with things about her woman's body she'd never known. Exactly the right place to touch. When to stroke, slide, dip or plunge. How absolutely arousing a slow, smooth hand could be. Their world became her only world.

'Ben…' She couldn't help the breathy little sounds coming from her throat, couldn't help arching blindly towards the source of that pleasure. But there was more; something just out of reach. Something her body instinctively sought. 'Ben, I want…I need…'

'I know.' The hot glide of his clever fingers over slick and swollen flesh increased. Darts shot through her body, lights exploded behind her eyes. Her body spasmed as her climax ripped through her, sending her to another dimension.

He was still there when she floated back to earth. Time drifted like the tide, the air hung heavy, languid, scented with desire.

Then he rolled away, reached for something on the night stand. She heard the rip of foil and closed her eyes as his weight settled over her. She felt his heart thundering against her breast, his breath hot against her ear, and prepared to be swept away.

But when the blunt tip of his sex nudged her, rosy dreams and soft sighs vanished, and reality intruded like a harsh white light. The magnitude of what she was doing hit her.

Too late. With one deep thrust that stole the air from her lungs, he pushed inside her, then went utterly still. And bit out a short four-letter word.

She tensed at the quick sharp pain and held her breath, trying not to panic. She felt impaled, his hardness invasive and foreign. Only his rapid and heavy breathing broke the silence.

'Why didn't you tell me?'

'You didn't ask.' She could barely speak, so focused was she on her own body and what was happening to her. Already the pain was subsiding, already she wanted more. Until an added vulnerability cooled her enthusiasm. Perhaps he didn't like virgins; perhaps the reason he was speaking in that harsh tone was because he was disappointed. 'Does it matter?'

'Too bloody right.' He carefully withdrew a little, propped himself on his elbows over her and dropped a sweat-damp forehead on hers. 'There are rules…'

'We…I…broke a rule coming here. You said—'

'*My* rules. There's a difference.' He traced a finger over her cheek, her lips. There was a myriad emotions in his eyes. 'Why now...why me?'

'Because I want it, because you're here. Please...' She grasped his hand, took it to her breast. 'Tonight you've made me feel beautiful and so alive.'

An infinitely more wary look crossed his face. 'Don't make this into something it's not, Carissa. I'm not that man of your dreams, nor am I a settling-down kind of guy. This is all there is.'

She swallowed and forced herself to remember how it was. 'This is all I want. I'm not looking for permanence. That makes us ideal partners for this evening.' She twined her arms around his neck and experimentally moved her hips.

His jaw tightened, his arms quivering with the strain of holding his weight off her. 'Look, Carissa, I don't want to hurt you...'

'Don't give me that sexist rubbish about it being different for a woman.' She raked her nails over his back and the hard curve of his buttocks, making him shudder.

'Well, then. You'll want something worth remembering.' His eyes darkened. '*That* I can give you.'

He was true to his word.

Hungry for his taste, his body and completion, she took what he gave greedily, storing the sensations and emotions for later. Dark, heavy heat engulfed her, molten fire flowing through her veins, spreading over her skin. Her body relaxed as she became familiar with him moving over and within her. She'd never forget this one time with him. He was everything she'd dreamed of and then some.

Strength. His body was hard and smooth against hers, tempered with a gentleness she hadn't expected.

Patience. Another surprise, his willingness to linger over small things—a touch, a kiss, a murmur.

Tenderness. It flowed from his touch like soft summer rain.

And when the ache built again and became unbearable, he knew, and let her fly.

After, he lay silent and still, holding her against him, but somehow removed. As if he'd distanced himself.

How it should be, she told herself. He'd be moving on and she'd go back to her two jobs, her falling-down house and her debts.

But rather than the satisfaction she'd expected, she felt… empty. And cheated somehow, as if she'd opened the door to another world and had it slammed in her face. And she still had to find a way out of his arms, out of this hotel and home—without being seen by management.

She hadn't meant to fall asleep. That was her first coherent thought when she woke to the unfamiliar weight of a hand on her abdomen. As she surfaced the night flooded back in a tide of exquisite sensations and images. For a fuzzy moment she drifted with them, aware of a vague tenderness in her lower body and a sense of togetherness she'd never experienced.

Then she blinked as her brain caught up. A grey-pearl sky heralded approaching dawn. A jolt of panic swept through her. Her reputation and job were at stake here. She fought the impulse to leap off the bed. Slow was the wisest course; the last thing she wanted to do was wake him.

She couldn't resist a last look. She'd never seen a naked man for real. Her moist, tender flesh throbbed at the sight of the thick jut of his sex, which seemed to augment as she watched. Her gaze shot to his face, but he was relaxed, long lashes resting on his cheeks.

Heart racing, she turned away. *Get out while you still can.* Easing her body out from under his arm was no mean feat, but he was dead to the world, his breathing calm and even.

Her stockings lay at the foot of the bed. She grabbed her bra and dress from the floor, hesitated before stuffing bra and stockings in her bag. She wriggled into the dress, jerked the zip up, then twisted her hair into its clasp while she searched for shoes.

Her panties were nowhere in sight, buried somewhere among the rumpled sheets or under that heavy, slumbering body. She had no intention of risking him waking, and counted the loss of a pair of knickers a minor one under the circumstances.

Then she noticed his wallet on the night stand. Money. Thank you, God. She hunted up pen and paper in her bag, wrote an IOU, promising him she'd reimburse him at the desk tomorrow, then slipped a bill into her purse. Couldn't be helped—he'd offered, and she absolutely, positively couldn't catch a train wearing nothing but an evening dress at six o'clock in the morning.

She looked longingly at the roses, but she couldn't take them. *Goodbye, Ben Jamieson.* She refused to look at him again as she stole from his room and out of his life.

Through barely raised eyelashes Ben watched her stumble quietly around his room. He'd lain awake the whole night afraid he'd succumb to his usual nightmare and scare her. And embarrass himself.

There was enough light to showcase the slender curves, the glint of gold at her ears and her shadowed secret places as she bent to find her clothes. She straightened, hesitated, giving him a close-up of those tempting globes of flesh with their dark puckered nipples.

Then she turned her back to him and slithered naked into her long blue tube, an innocent striptease in rewind. His blood heated, his already hardened sex turned painful and he had an irresistible urge to lay his lips on that moon-pale patch of skin above the swell of her bottom. Then she yanked the zip up and the moment was lost. Probably just as well.

He wondered if she intended catching her train at this hour, in that state of dress, and what he was going to do about it. He was relieved when he saw her write something on a scrap of paper, then slide a single furtive bill from his wallet. She could have robbed him blind. The fact that she didn't only confirmed what he already knew. Carissa was an honest if naïve young woman.

Her movements ruffled the air so that her scent wafted to his nose. Not an expensive perfume, but a scent that made him think of a spring morning—cool, fresh, unspoiled. Maybe she was too embarrassed to face him—she'd obviously never done the morning-after routine. It beat the hell out of him why a woman would opt for a stranger for her first sexual experience.

He watched her leave his room and head for the elevator, then stretched, punched up the pillow and shoved his hands behind his head. The trouble with virgins—one intimate encounter and they started looking at engagement rings. Carissa was different.

He heard the elevator doors open, close, and felt more alone than he'd felt before he'd met her. As if she'd taken part of him. Which was plain stupid. No woman took anything from Ben Jamieson.

Throwing off the sheet, he padded to the window to catch a glimpse of her. There. He watched her hail a cab, climb in and drive away. His fists clenched on the window ledge. Damn her for making him feel…needy. He didn't want to get involved. Not with her, not with anyone. And not now, when his life was going down the toilet.

Moving to his bed, he reached into his jeans pocket and pulled out the slender gold chain he'd slipped off her wrist. Antique, by the looks. Insurance, he told himself, pocketing it once more. He could see her again if he wanted, if he chose to. He knew where she was on a Friday and Saturday night. Simple.

Or he could keep it even simpler. *Just Carissa,* an intimate stranger who'd shared his bed for a night. Some soft curves in the bumpy road that was his life right now.

She didn't know he had her bracelet. And her panties, he noted, spotting the scrap of blue silk on the bed amongst the tumbled sheets. Ah well, he'd have them gift wrapped and handed in to her at the front desk. But he'd see she got the bracelet back personally.

A girl with her classical background wouldn't know anything about a band like XLRock, he decided, hunting up a room-service menu. Rave's band had needed financial backing to get started and Ben had been happy to put down the money.

Fourteen years ago in a tiny pub on the edge of the Nullabor Plain, Ben had taken the fifteen-year-old runaway pickpocket under his wing and taught him to play guitar. The kid had become a runaway star.

Ben stared sightlessly at the ceiling. All he saw was Rave. A couple of weeks ago he'd stepped in with his own guitar to help out when one of the band members had quit on the eve of the open-air concert, Desert Rock. But Ben hadn't been able to resist the lure of Broken Hill's Musicians' Club on the way home.

The memory taunted him. His stomach tied itself into those familiar knots and he decided he wasn't hungry after all. Grimly he grabbed his jeans from the floor where he'd shucked them last night and headed for the shower.

Adjusting the temperature to just above cold, he let the water pelt him and shivered as he soaped up. He could still see the frustration in Rave's eyes. But he'd grown accustomed to the tantrums. 'Jess won't mind one extra night, Rave. Phone her and blame me. Here, take the Porsche for a spin.' He'd handed him the car keys himself.

It was the last time he'd seen him.

Ben wrenched off the taps, pressed his fingers to his eyelids. He hadn't expected Rave to be irresponsible enough to get plastered before he got behind the wheel. He should have seen it. He'd tried to escape the visions that plagued him—waking, sleeping—but the guilt stuck like barbed wire.

And the nightmares kept coming.

For one brief evening, Carissa had made him forget.

When he re-entered the main room, the *Sydney Morning Herald* had been slipped beneath the door by some faceless night porter. Without glancing at the headlines he tossed it into the bin. He was so tired of the smell of impersonal hotel rooms. Sick of the sight of staff with their plastic smiles, the clatter of service trolleys.

He turned to the spectacular view of high-rises against a gold sky. Just once he wanted to look out a window and see an untidy cottage garden or a stand of stringy eucalypts, a wooden letter-box with the paint peeling off. How many years had it been since he'd slept in a house? A home? Too damn many.

He needed a place where no one who knew him could find him. Space where he could think for a few days before the gut-wrenching prospect of facing up to Jess.

Even if he had to pay a couple of months' rent for a few days, the room on Sydney's coast advertised in the staff cafeteria might just be the temporary hideaway he was looking for.

CHAPTER THREE

SLIDING his sunglasses down his nose, Ben studied the house from his hire car, checked the ad again. 'Want a quiet retreat away from city noise?' it read. 'Spacious old family home. Own bed/sitting/bathroom, share kitchen. Meals cooked if preferred.'

The house itself was a gracious old bungalow but someone had let it go. The midday sun glared off a khaki lawn and a row of straggling rose bushes. Faded paintwork was peeling along the verandah and around the windows. The roof sagged and one of the wooden steps leading to the front door was missing.

Mozart—at least he thought it was—drifted through an open window as he unfolded himself and climbed out of the car. He pushed open the gate, caught the scents of coffee and fresh-baked cake as he walked up the path.

He knocked and a voice sounded from somewhere inside. The door opened and a young woman with a long flow of black hair and grey eyes looked out. Her skimpy olive crop-top revealed smooth tanned skin. Black Lycra shorts clung to shapely legs. She was, in a word, a knockout.

'Good morning, my name's Ben Jamieson. I've come about the room.'

She stared at him a moment, then her mouth curved into a wide grin. 'Hey, Carrie, your piano tuner's here,' she called in an amused voice to someone down the passage.

'No,' he began, 'there's some misunderstanding, the room—'

'Ben Jamieson.' Her eyes narrowed. 'Wait up. *The* Ben Jamieson?' She grinned. 'I'm Melanie Sawyer, Carrie's stepsister.' She offered her hand, her grip firm. 'I just called round on my way home from the hospital—I'm a nurse.'

'I didn't ring for a piano tuner, and the kitchen sink...' A woman joined Melanie, her voice trailing off when she saw him.

His blue lady transformed.

Biting back the first word that sprang to his lips, he exhaled sharply, rocked back on his heels.

'Carrie, there you are,' Melanie said. 'This is Ben Jamieson. He's come about the room. Ben, this is—'

'Carissa.'

He compared the two females, both gazes fixed on him. Melanie might dazzle the eye, but Carissa shone with an inner spark that set her apart.

Right now her hair was an out-of-control waterfall of gold. A buttercup-yellow vest-top clung to braless breasts. Mile-long legs gleamed beneath short denim cut-offs and she had two dark stains on her knees and a glob of something black on her cheek. Her feet were bare.

She didn't look pleased to see him.

Her cheeks flushed but those blue eyes turned a dangerous shade of cool. 'What are you doing here?'

'I was in the staff cafeteria...' He held out the ad.

Her eyes narrowed. 'How did you manage that?'

'Friends in high places?' He should just get the hell away, but he couldn't seem to move his feet.

Melanie frowned. 'You know each other?'

'I don't...' Carissa threw him a suspicious look, then turned to her sister. 'How do *you* know him?'

Melanie shook her head at Ben. 'The queen of pop, Carrie is not. Ben's a songwriter.' Her brow creased. 'You were there when...oh, God.' Her sentence hung in an awkward silence broken only by the chattering of birds and Mozart pouring from the stereo inside. 'Rave Elliot, XLRock,' she finished in a low voice.

Carissa's eyes widened and thawed to lukewarm. 'That horrific accident. I read about it.' She leaned a shoulder against the door. Not flushed now but pale as milk. 'I had no idea you… I'm sorry. For your loss.'

The pain struck hard. 'Rave and I were like brothers.'

For a few hours this woman had taken his mind off his grief. Not just with her body, but with charm and optimism. Could she be good for him a little longer? If they laid the ground rules from the start…

He took a fortifying breath. His best decisions were often ones he didn't think about too deeply. 'I'd like to look at the room.'

But Carissa frowned. 'Why? Why would you choose a cheap rented room over a penthouse suite?'

A fair question. 'I need a private place for a while. If you're worried about the short stay, I'm happy to pay you six months' rent up front.'

The frown remained.

Melanie flashed him a reassuring smile. 'Excuse us a moment. Wait right here,' she said, tugging Carissa inside and pushing the door to.

He paced a couple of steps away and considered the wisdom of his offer. Carissa obviously didn't want him here and he—

'Ben?'

He turned at the sound of Melanie's voice.

Carissa stood beside her, flicking one hand against her thigh and looking aggrieved. He saw her throat bob as she swallowed, then she nodded. 'Okay, you can take a look.'

'So, how did you two meet?' Ben heard Melanie ask.

Carissa swallowed again. 'The piano bar. We had a drink…'

Knowing eyes met his, deep ocean-blue, and he had a mental flashback of that long, slender body laid out and arching beneath him. 'Which reminds me.' He dug into his pocket. 'I have something of yours.'

'Oh, no...don't...I...' She did a quick embarrassed shuffle.

He took his time, watching the way her eyes darkened, heated, pleaded, then chilled. 'You must've dropped this.'

'Oh...my— Thank God.' Pink and flustered again now, she made no move to take the gold chain he held in front of her eyes.

He cocked a brow. 'You sound surprised. Have you lost something else?'

Her eyes skittered to Mel, then away, and she seemed to fight a little war within herself before the glare was back, the chin up. Ignoring his last question, she opened her hand, palm out. 'It was my grandmother's. I only discovered I wasn't wearing it this morning.'

His fingers grazed hers as he poured it into her hand. He lingered over them a second before she snatched them away.

'The room's this way, Mr Jamieson,' she said, all business as she turned and headed down the passage. 'The upkeep of the room is the tenant's responsibility. There's no room service here.'

'Carrie,' Melanie scolded, bringing up the rear. She cast an apologetic glance at Ben. 'She's not been herself all morning. I don't know what's gotten into her.'

He almost smiled. Was this the same woman who'd melted— burned—in his arms last night? That fragrance, her cool blue water scent that had enveloped him like a misty morning, was tantalising him again, reminding him of the passion he'd woken in her. Only him. The thought persisted a little longer than he'd have liked.

It was an airy house with only the basics, and echoes of a time when it had looked different. They passed a couple of empty rooms, then entered a spacious area that must have been used for entertaining. A piano filled the space by a huge bay window. Sheet music was scattered over the lid; some lay in a cardboard box. A tatty sofa, a couple of sagging chairs and a coffee-table were the only furniture.

He wished she'd stop, wished Melanie would get lost so he

and Carissa could talk, but she strode on, long legs flashing beneath those skimpy shorts.

'Careful,' she warned at the kitchen door. 'Sink's blocked.'

Which explained the black knees. They trod carefully over the slippery floor. 'You called the plumber?'

Melanie let out a hoot, which earned her a black look from Carissa.

'I'll take a look—' he began.

Carissa waved him off. 'Got it covered.' A phone rang. 'Can you answer that, Mel, please, and tell whoever I'll call back?' She pushed at a door. 'These are the rooms. Not up to your usual standard, I'm sure, so—'

'I'll take it,' he said, without bothering to look. He preferred watching the conflicting emotions play over her face. 'Hold still,' he murmured, flicking the drop from her cheek with his thumb. 'A spot of drain dew. Gunk,' he clarified when she just stared at him.

She touched her cheek. 'This is *not* happening.'

He cocked a brow. 'Think of it as a coincidence.'

'I believe in signs, not coincidences, Mr Jamieson.'

'A sign, then.' Of what, he wasn't sure. Stretching a lazy arm across the doorframe, he foiled her getaway. 'What's with the Mr Jamieson? We've seen each other naked. Shouldn't we be informal?' He watched her colour flare and gentled his voice. 'We need to talk, Carissa.'

'If you're referring to last night, there's nothing to talk about. Anything else is purely business, *Mr* Jamieson.' Her voice was crisp and edgy. She started to push past, then stopped, obviously unwilling to touch him.

He saved her the trouble, curling his fingers loosely around her arm. The faintest tremor ran through her. 'I think there is. I'm making you uncomfortable. If we're going to be living together we need—'

'I haven't decided yet whether or not to take you on. And *if* I do, we will *not* be living together.'

'Okay,' he conceded. '*If* you decide I'm the right man for the job, we're inevitably going to be in each other's space. I don't want you uncomfortable in your own home.'

He was all too aware of the smooth skin beneath his palm. He was trying to reassure, but it was too tempting to remember her flesh sliding against his. Damn, but he wanted that feeling again.

'I'm a good bet, Carissa. You don't want someone you know nothing about coming into your house.'

'And I know you?' she said wryly. She chewed her lips a moment. 'Okay, we'll give it a go, but I'm not making any long-term deals.'

'I'm not looking for long term.' He cruised his hand up that slender neck, felt the rapid pulse, the shallow breathing. His gaze dropped to that full mouth and he watched it tremble before it firmed. Proud and defensive. He liked that in a woman. 'Carissa...'

'A one-night stand, that's all,' she whispered, her eyes pleading with his.

Ironic that he'd echoed those same sentiments until it was second nature to him. 'Seems fate has other ideas.'

'No.' She swung away, stubbing her toes on a chair in her haste. 'Ouch!' Her face turned waxy pale.

'Ouch,' he echoed with feeling.

Clutching her foot, she staggered to the nearest available surface, a sofa with a bright hand-quilted throw-over. 'Fudge, fudge, fudge!'

Ready to render first aid whether she needed it or not, he crossed the room and knelt in front of her. 'Let's take a look.'

'It's fine. Great. No, really.'

Her foot jerked, but he grasped her heel before she could pull away. It was smudged with dirt, the toenails painted silver. One nail was broken and bleeding. He whipped out a handkerchief and wiped away the blood, but his thumb slid back and forth over her cool, smooth instep of its own volition.

The urge to slide his hand on up that firm calf muscle, and

higher, beat through his blood. His body hardened. Living under her roof might be more difficult than he'd anticipated. He looked up at her. Her teeth were worrying her lip again, a provocative sight if he ever saw one. He could press his advantage, or act like a gentleman, which he wasn't.

But he let her go. 'Okay, Cinderella, I think you'll live.' Shoving his handkerchief in his pocket, he walked to the window, willing his inconvenient erection to subside.

This bed-cum-sitting room was better furnished than what he'd seen of the rest of the house, with a view overlooking the rear grounds, *grounds* being the operative word.

Filmy white curtains moved in the breeze, another handmade quilt in maroon and cream covered a single bed. The rug on the floor was new, the pine floor freshly lacquered. He could still smell polish, disinfectant and sunshine on the fabrics.

'There's no air-conditioning, but you've a fan,' she said, still hugging her foot. 'Bathroom's through there.'

He took the opportunity while inspecting the sixties-style green and black room to moisten a dainty embroidered towel. 'This is a beautiful old house,' he said, offering her the cloth.

'I think so. Thanks, but I'm okay.' She folded it neatly and put it on the table in front of her. 'It was my grandparents' home. I've had to let things go a little. Upkeep on a place like this costs an arm and a leg, but I don't want to sell. It's all I have left of my family.'

'That's tough,' he said, and meant it. He knew all too well about losing the people you loved.

'I do just fine on my own.' The unconscious lift of her chin told him she had to work hard at it. It was obvious she needed money.

She glanced at her watch. 'I have to go out for a while. There's cake and coffee in the kitchen. Don't use the sink. You're free to use the kitchen, but the rest of the house is private, just as I'll respect your privacy. That way we can keep out of each other's hair.'

'Okay.' He nodded, but keeping his hands out of that tangle of gold was going to be a serious exercise in restraint.

She pushed up. 'I'll be back in time to cook tea, if you want to settle in.' She slid open a drawer, took out a set of keys and put them on the table. 'Back and front doors. And you can park that bomb you call a car in the garage; it's empty for now.'

'Hey, that's a fine car. Paintwork's a bit dodgy but the engine's reliable—so they tell me. We'll have to take a drive some time, see if they're up to their word.'

She didn't reply to that, but knotted her fingers at her waist. 'Rent's payable up front, two weeks in advance.' She paused, and twin spurts of colour sprang to her cheekbones. 'And, please, knock off the money I borrowed this morning. I intended to drop it off at the hotel.'

'No,' he said quietly, drawing out his wallet. He counted the notes and held them out. 'It's yours.'

'Okay. Thanks…um, Ben.' She took them, carefully avoiding contact with his hand.

He was tempted to cuff her wrist and test the beat of her pulse, but thought better of it. Business was business.

As she closed the door behind her he pulled out his keys. He'd head back to the city and grab his gear. Then maybe he'd take a stroll to the beach, a few minutes' walk away from here, and make some short-term plans.

Plans that might or might not include Carissa Grace.

As expected, Melanie leapt off the couch with a 'Wow!' the moment Carissa entered the living room.

'Yeah. Wow,' Carissa mimicked less enthusiastically as she snatched up a fabric band from the piano and dragged her hair through it. 'Who was on the phone?' she asked as casually as she could manage.

'Didn't say. I told him you were out, said he'd ring back. So, come on, Carrie, you were going to knock back his offer, for goodness' sake. You wouldn't say no to the extra income from a gorgeously handsome guy. What's going on with you two?'

Her stomach jittered. 'Nothing's "going on".'

'Don't give me that. I saw the way he looked at you. Hot.'

'I didn't notice.' She glared at Melanie, but she could still feel that flash of heat on her skin. 'Wipe that smirk off your face.' It was making her nervous. She could feel her face flaming, so she began collecting the scattered sections of yesterday's newspaper.

'The piano tuner?' Melanie murmured.

'Stop it, Mel.'

'Okay, but look at the points in his favour. He's a hunk, you have to agree.' She held up her fingers as she checked them off. 'He's available, he must be loaded, he's here—'

'That's just it,' Carissa interrupted. 'He's *here*. If I wanted a one-night stand, would I choose my lodger? Someone I see day in, day out?' And felt hot all over again.

'I don't know—would you?'

Carissa looked up to see Mel's eyebrows arched and a speculative gleam in her eyes. 'And five, he's interested. You want someone to tickle your ar…peggio—he's a songwriter and musician. What better credentials?'

'I don't know why I'm still talking to you, but stay for tea, Mel. Help me out here.'

Mel shook her head, setting her long hair swinging. 'You don't need any help from me, sis. And Adam and I made plans to go bowling tonight.'

'Bring your sexy and *available* flatmate too. The more the merrier.' And safer.

'Not tonight. You're on your own with this one.'

'Traitor,' Carissa muttered, tossing the paper on the coffee-table and throwing herself onto the couch.

Melanie grinned, picked up her bag and swung it over her shoulder. 'You'll thank me later. Gotta go.' But she paused at the door. 'You're not still thinking about Alasdair, are you? If you want to talk, I'm always free, or if you want to kick something, Adam's available.'

Carissa couldn't help smiling back. 'I'll tell Adam you offered him. And, no, I'm not thinking of Alasdair.'

When Melanie had gone, Carissa slapped on her floppy old hat and stepped out into the zap of a white summer's afternoon. The heat seared her exposed skin and baked the ground to biscuit, burning the soles of her worn sandals.

She welcomed the distraction. First up he'd walked into her piano bar. What were the odds of that same man walking into her home? Her life? She lifted the sprigs of lavender and rosemary she'd picked from her miniature herb patch, inhaling their calming scent as she walked.

She wanted alone. She liked alone. The desperate need for money was the only motivation for letting some of the spare rooms, not any desire for company. Now she had someone she neither needed nor wanted in her space.

Well, he wouldn't follow her here. A row of tired casuarinas shaded the tiny graveyard behind the old church. The gate registered her arrival with a mournful screech of rusted metal. She walked straight to her grandmother's grave.

'Hi, Gran.' She arranged the herbs in the earthenware pot, then sat, tossing her hat to the ground beside her. Her father and Mel's mother's grave lay a couple of rows away. Her own mother had been out of Carissa's life longer than she could remember.

She'd been visiting her grandmother's grave for fourteen years. It was Gran she talked to when she wanted to get something off her chest. No one interrupted here. She made important decisions under these trees. Solved problems, answered questions.

The peace of the hot afternoon lay over her like a languid blanket. Closing her eyes, she tuned her senses to her surroundings. The kiss of warm air on her skin, the scent of herbs and casuarina needles, the drone of a plane.

She opened her eyes and traced the grooves of her grandmother's name. 'Gran, I've done something I'm not sure you'd approve of. I met a man.' She found her heart thudding louder and rubbed the heel of her hand over it. 'You know the type—tall, dark and deliciously dangerous. We had a drink and I gave him my virginity. I'd known him an hour.'

She clasped her hands around her knees, conscious of her breathing, a little faster than usual, skin newly sensitised, the tingling in her breasts as the memories flowed back, clear and fluid.

'And you know what else? I'm not ashamed of it. Even knowing there'll never be anything between us. He didn't seduce me. I went in with my eyes wide open. *I* used *him,* knowing I'd never see him again. How's that for women's rights? Except now…now he's living under my roof.' She heard the tremble in her own voice and stood up.

'The moment I saw him standing at my door it was all I could do not to lay my lips on his and take.' She shoved her hands in the pockets of her shorts and frowned at the ground. 'But that's not going to happen, I made it quite clear. I think.'

A car whizzed by, a blur of sound. The air stirred, thick and heavy with summer scents.

'How am I going to face him over the kitchen table knowing what we've done?' Her head suddenly filled with Ben's face, his eyes on hers as he drove into her. Her body writhing beneath his, her shameless moans…

She shook it away, clenched her fists. 'Alasdair's got someone else.' Her lip curled. '*Pierre.* I thought I'd feel hurt but I feel used and angry. I was counting on his financial support. He'd promised to fix up the house. It was going to be my turn to study at the conservatorium.' She blew out a breath. 'I've realised I'm more upset at the loss of his income than the man himself. We had a good partnership. Now I realise that's all it was.

'So I had no choice but to rent those rooms. It was supposed to be temporary, but now it's vital. I'll keep your house, Gran, if it's the last thing I do.

'And Ben Jamieson's going to help me pay for it.

'He likes rock, for heaven's sake. We're worlds apart.' She

bent, picked up her hat, then kissed her fingers and touched the headstone. And sighed as a smile curved her mouth. 'But I haven't felt so alive in for ever.'

CHAPTER FOUR

BEN spent a quiet half hour unloading his gear. It felt good tripping up the rickety front steps, hearing the squeak of the porch screen door. If Carissa had no objections he might put his energy to productive use and fix the place up a bit, bring the garden back to life.

As he set his laptop and paperwork on the tiny desk in his room he noticed the homey touches. The dish of pot-pourri, a handmade candle that smelled of vanilla, the embroidered pillowslip and tissue-box cover.

Twenty-four hours ago he'd never met Carissa Grace; now he was living in her house. He stared at the ad still on the table. What twist of fate had led him to that notice-board yesterday? Was this one of those mystical signs Carissa believed in? He sure as eggs didn't believe in that mumbo jumbo.

So why did he have this odd niggly feeling in his gut?

To distract himself, he wandered to the kitchen, found a vase for the roses he'd brought from the hotel, put them on the table. Next he picked up the tools Carissa had left and inspected the sink. So she was a plumber too. He wasn't, but he was prepared to give it a try.

Half an hour, a bruised elbow and a few curses later he had the drain flowing freely—he hoped. He let himself out the back door and hunted up a hose on top of a pile of cracked pots in an old garden shed. She obviously didn't find time for gardening, which was a crying shame. The garden could be quite spectacular with a little time and effort.

He'd never had a backyard of his own. The simple pleasure of pottering around in your own garden, watching it grow, was not something he'd ever given much thought to. He connected the hose and soon had the water playing over what he imagined had once been lawn. He wasn't sure it could be revived, but he'd give it his best shot.

The activity reminded him of his mother. Her garden had been her pride and joy. His gut tightened at the memory. Even then she'd been lost. At sixteen he'd been too focused on himself to look at what was going on around him—he'd just known he wanted out of there.

He'd come back four years later and been shocked at what he'd discovered his drunken father had been doing. But she'd refused to go to the women's shelter he'd arranged, refused to return with him to the outback pub he'd been working in at the time. Still, the guilt that he'd had to leave her with the bastard remained like a wound that never healed.

'What are you doing?' The steel in Carissa's voice had a red-hot edge to it.

He turned to see her marching across the yard towards him, hat in hand, eyes blazing. 'Giving the lawn a helping hand,' he said. 'Looks like it needs it.'

'And who appointed you gardener?'

He couldn't resist. He adjusted the nozzle to a fine spray and grinned. 'You look a little hot and bothered. Let's cool you off.'

'Don't—' She gasped as the fine mist enveloped her.

Her hat sailed into the dust. Water sparkled on her shoulders, in her hair. She didn't look cooled off at all. He wondered that the water didn't turn to steam, she looked so darn angry.

'Turn it off. Now.'

When he just stood watching in fascination, she renewed her march, this time towards the tap. He moved to intercept her.

Her fingers closed over his as she struggled for the hose, drenching them. 'Stop it!'

Mud spattered their feet. The smell of wet earth rose around them as her breasts rubbed against his chest. She pulled back, her T-shirt plastered to her body, her pebbled nipples jutting up at him.

'Now look what you've done,' she muttered, swiping her face.

Oh, yeah. He was looking.

Then for just a moment laughter bubbled up, bright and sunny and uninhibited. 'This'll cost you, Mr Jamieson.'

The hose slipped to the ground, spraying water over their feet. 'Tack it onto the rent.'

'I was thinking along the line of no showers for a week. Teach you a lesson in water conservation.'

'Then I'd be forced to share yours.'

Her eyes shot laser-bright blue sparks as he hauled her up against him. He felt the exasperation sing through her arm as she pushed at his chest, relished it as he tugged her back against him. It had been a while since he'd enjoyed a tussle with a woman, even if he'd have preferred somewhere more horizontal.

'What's the problem, Miz Grace, afraid of a little water?' Silky legs rubbed against his and he shifted to take advantage. Something about this woman called to him. Her vitality, her innocence? It was more than physical, although his physical needs took precedence at this moment.

Everywhere her body touched him came alive. He knew she felt his erection when she tensed and went very still. That knowledge and the taut, unspoken silence hummed in his ears, beat through his blood. He lowered his mouth until it was an intimate suggestion away from hers. 'Or are you afraid of something else?'

Her eyes snapped shut. 'I'm *afraid* the water's wasting. I'm *afraid* when the water bill comes I won't be able to pay. So now you know, turn off the tap.'

It cost her to admit that, and he eased back. 'Is that why you let the garden go?' he asked softly.

Diamond drops clung to her lashes, her pretty mouth was a thin line. 'You think I like a baked yard?' She shook her head, scattering droplets.

'I apologise.' Reluctantly he disentangled his body from hers and stepped away to shut off the tap. He wanted to help, but knew her pride wouldn't allow her to accept cash. He'd have to find another way.

He didn't expect her to be right behind him picking up her hat when he turned. His foot slipped as he tried to compensate and they slid to the ground in a slow-motion pinwheel of thrashing limbs and hot skin. He heard her strangled cry, felt the cool sensation of damp earth rise up to meet them as he frantically twisted his body to take the brunt of the fall.

He ended up on his back, Carissa's legs around his waist, her breasts fragrant pillows against his nose.

Her moan—or was it his?—sounded through his muffled senses as his hands reached up and clamped on firm buttocks. She squirmed, one nipple brushing his face, his mouth. He acted on instinct, turning his cheek and closing his lips around the hard little bud beneath the cotton.

With a startled yelp she pushed up instantly, giving him a tantalising close-up of wet T-shirt. Wet, *transparent* T-shirt with a puckered circle where his mouth had been.

He tipped his head back. Stunned wide and aware eyes met his. Fingers of lust seared his veins and clutched his groin. Wordlessly he slid his hands to her hips and dragged her body lower so that she sat poised over him. Pain or pleasure? He wasn't sure, didn't care.

Her hands splayed over his chest. 'No,' she breathed, a throaty sound that echoed through his head and over his body, but her fingers bunched and twisted into his vest-top, her knuckles dragged over his nipples. God.

He loosened his grip briefly to give her the opportunity of escape. She remained frozen in place, the only movement the rise and fall of her breasts as he flexed his fingers against her again.

He traced the long, smooth muscles at the front of her thighs, let his thumbs curve inwards and upwards to the hem of her shorts, until he found the lacy edge of her panties.

Her quick indrawn gasp turned his body to fire. Her focus blurred, her lips parted as he slid his thumbs beneath the lace to find her hot and wet. Guilt stabbed through him when he remembered how he'd taken her innocence last night.

He drew in a harsh controlled breath. 'Are you sore?' he murmured, hearing the sandpaper rasp of his own voice as he explored deeper, hearing her moan as he rubbed his thumb over the engorged knot of flesh.

'No...oh.' Colour flared up her neck and into her cheeks. 'This isn't working,' she muttered thickly.

He cocked a disbelieving brow, tugged on the crotch of her panties and slid the knuckles of one hand back and forth over her delicious heat. 'It's not?'

She moaned, her head dropping forward so that her hair brushed his shoulders. 'You...offered to...cool me off.'

'This is more fun.' Absolutely, definitely... Except... He inhaled her incredible female scent as he absorbed the wet heat against his fingers and tried like hell to ignore the insistent pounding of his own need to roll on top of her and plunge inside.

No condoms.

He touched her again, once, and she came apart, her body arching, then melting down onto him with a satisfied moan. An experience he wasn't going to get any time soon.

Then her gaze locked on his. The dreamy focus sharpened as his body jerked against her. *Hell.* In one not-so-smooth motion he rolled her off him and sat up.

'You don't wa...?'

Oh, yeah, he did. Right now he wanted it more than his next breath, but he didn't do unprotected sex. No woman was going to trap him with an unwanted pregnancy.

A shower—he needed that shower. Cold. Alone. Now. 'That's

enough for one day,' he muttered through his teeth. 'You're new at this. Bound to be a bit tender.'

To distract himself from the soft, puzzled look in her eyes and the erotic scent of her sex on his fingers, he reached out beside him and picked up her hat.

'Looks like we both need that shower,' he said, looking at their damp, dirt-stained clothes. *Not* looking at her breasts and crotch. 'Then we could eat out, get some take-away. My shout.'

We. Without his being aware of even saying it, his heart tightened and something inside him needed.

Suddenly the scenario seemed way too domestic. If he wasn't careful, that need to be a part of someone's life, to share their day, could spring to life again as easily as the brown grass beneath his feet.

He needn't have worried. Averting her eyes, she swiped at her knees with tense, jerky movements, but he saw the telling blush that stained her cheeks.

'It's my night off,' she said, her voice husky. 'I'm going to the movies with a girlfriend.'

A lie, he knew. 'Hey,' he said quietly, and stood up. He lifted her chin with a finger and looked into those wide blue eyes still shiny with the afterglow of sex. 'It's okay. You don't have to leave your house on my account. I've got some work to take care of in my room. I'll grab myself a snack later.'

He shook the dust off her hat, set it on her head, then turned and walked to the house. But he felt her eyes on him all the way to the back door.

'You were seen exiting the employee entrance at dawn in a less than seemly state, Ms Grace. The Cove Hotel will not tolerate such shameful behaviour from its employees.'

The scents of the summer evening filled the air. Carissa hardly noticed as she clutched the phone in front of the open kitchen window. Angry humiliation stung her eyes. Once. She'd made one tiny indiscretion. Okay, not so tiny. 'I'm sorry, Mr Christos.' For the sake of her job, she swallowed her pride and said, 'I let the Cove down. It won't happen again.'

'No, it will not. I want to see you in my office tomorrow morning at 9:00 a.m.'

'I'll be there.'

She stabbed the disconnect button and slammed the phone down, then banged her forehead against the kitchen cupboard. 'Jerk!' How many more surprises could she take today?

'Your boss?'

She whirled at the deep voice to see Ben at the door, hair still damp from his shower, one hand on the door-frame.

A hand that had only a few hours ago wreaked devastation on her body with one expert glide between her spread legs. Good Lord. Heat spurted into her cheeks; her heart hammered in her chest. But now he was witnessing a different kind of devastation. 'How long have you been there?'

'Long enough to get the drift.'

'I see.' And obviously, so did he. Humiliated, embarrassed and determined to ignore him, she marched to the pantry and pulled out ingredients. She dumped flour and salt into a bowl, then added a generous squirt of blue food colouring and stirred till her arm ached. Anything to avoid looking at him.

He pushed away from the door. 'If that's supper, I'll pass.'

'Thought you were going to fix your own.'

'Thought you were going to the movies.'

Oh. 'My friend cancelled.' She wiped her brow with the back of her hand. 'It's play dough.'

'Kid stuff play dough?'

'For the kids at the hospital. Mel often helps out in the children's cancer ward.' She put the bowl in the microwave, set the timer. Watched the turntable. Ben sat—obviously he'd finished whatever work he had—and made himself comfortable.

When the timer dinged, she scooped the hot dough into a ball, then carried it to the table and set it beside the fragrant bouquet Ben had put there. 'I haven't thanked you for bringing the roses back. So thank you. I love them.' Even if they were a reminder of an evening best forgotten. Hell, a reminder of a whole twenty-four hours.

'You're welcome.'

'Try this.' She broke off a piece of dough for Ben, then sank her fingers in and began to knead. 'I love the texture, and when it's warm... Someone reported me.'

Ben rolled his dough between his palms. 'I'll make a call—'

'No. Definitely not.' She almost snorted. As if he could do anything. No way was she letting him get involved in her problems.

'So we'll take a drive,' he said. 'Blow away some of the day's stresses. Give me five minutes.'

Tempting. It was a genuine offer of support and she sure needed a change of scenery. 'You said you had work.'

'It's not going anywhere.' He leaned over, lifted her chin with a finger and their eyes met. 'For the record, whatever last night was, it wasn't a mistake.' Something in his gaze shifted, darkened, as the full-frontal memories of hot and heavy and wet rose between them.

She squeezed the dough till it oozed between her fingers. 'I'm fine. It's going to be fine.' After all, optimism was supposed to be her strong point.

He set his ball of dough on the table beside her hand. 'Of course it will.'

Yeah. He would think that. The complete confidence of a man who had everything. A man who didn't understand what it was like to go without—anything.

'One condition,' she said, not looking at him. 'No sex.'

She felt the air stir as he stepped away. 'Whatever you say.'

They drove with the windows down as fast as the car could safely go until Sydney's lights were only a glow on the horizon.

'You have a destination in mind?' Melbourne, perhaps?

'I'll know when we get there.'

He tuned into a rock station playing nineties party hits. 'Guess it's not your thing, huh?' he said after a few moments.

'Just because I play classical doesn't mean I don't like other music.'

'Guitar?' he asked.

'I love guitar. Spanish, classical...'

Ben nodded. 'Classical guitar's the only "classical" I know much about.'

'And now a hit from XLRock's latest album...' The DJ's voice faded and the guitar riff slid out of the tinny speakers.

Without warning, Ben punched the radio off. Only the sounds of wind and engine filled the silence. He stared ahead, his clenched jaw reflecting the sombre green dashboard lighting. He could have been carved from stone.

'I'm sorry,' Carissa said, wishing she knew how to ease his hurt.

Ignoring her miserable attempt, he pulled over near a flat, almost treeless expanse of land. 'Let's walk,' he said tautly.

Away from the city's glare, the sky was brilliant indigo and full of stars. A full moon rode above low hills on the horizon. Cricket song and buzzing insects filled the air. The calming sounds and soothing sights went some way to easing the awkward tension.

'Know your stars?' he asked, finally. Some of the strain had gone from his voice.

'I know the Southern Cross.' She looked up at the familiar kite shape. 'And there's the Saucepan.'

He nodded. 'The constellation of Orion. And that bright one's Sirius. See the big red one? That's Betelgeuse. Have you ever seen the outback night sky?'

'I've never been more than a couple hundred kilometres from Sydney.'

'You should see it some day.' His eyes glittered with the reflected starlight as he gazed up. 'All that black emptiness. Makes you feel small and insignificant. Like we don't count for much in the big picture.'

'Or it fills you with wonder, knowing there must be a purpose behind it all.'

He looked at her, a half smile on his lips. 'Spoken like a true optimist.' He found a spot where the grass was flat, sat down and patted the space beside him. 'What do you want to do about your gig at the Cove?'

She blew out a disgusted breath. 'What *can* I do? I'm at old Georgie Christos's mercy.'

'I'm responsible. Let me—'

'No way. No way.' She shook her head. 'I stand on my own two feet. *I'm* responsible for me. I made a choice. I'll live with the consequences.' Whatever they might be. And it wasn't only her job she was thinking of.

'I don't want to work in a place where loyalty counts for nothing. If I lose it I'll live with it.' But she thought of the overdue bills on her desk and wondered if she was being stupid knocking back Ben's offer. 'I've still got my Monday to Thursday waitressing at the Three Steps. I'll ask them if they've got any Friday and Saturday shifts.'

'Waiting tables? You're wasted.' He angled towards her. 'I want to see you again at the piano in that blue number you wore last night.' His eyes barely flicked down, then met hers again. 'Better still, at the piano *not* in that blue number.

'Sorry, out of line,' he said immediately, pressing a finger to her lips, presumably to silence any complaints. She didn't have any. She did have an insane urge to take that finger into her mouth and wrap her tongue around it. To taste him again, to have a part of him inside her.

Oh, no. *No, no, no.* She couldn't let it happen again. And they'd made that sensible no-sex rule.

But she couldn't move. In the light of the rising moon his face was silver and shadows, his eyes still focused on hers. Then she felt the warm glide of his hand over her collar-bone, beneath the tiny strap on her shoulder. Her stomach tightened, her nipples hardened and that newly discovered sweet, deep pull tugged at her lower body.

'Don't. Please,' she begged, her throat dry, her voice suddenly hoarse. 'You promised.'

He didn't remove his hand. 'It's a guy, right? A guy lets you down, a one-night stand—classic rebound.'

She hesitated, then nodded. 'You must think I'm a fool.'

'No.' He tightened his grip on her shoulder and rubbed his thumb over her skin. 'He didn't deserve you, Carissa. And neither did I.'

'Let's get something straight here. I didn't offer myself to you like some sort of sacrifice. Don't you get it? I used you to—'

'Scratch an itch?' His lips curved in the dimness. 'We all do that at some time or other. But pick a man, any man? That's downright dangerous and *that's* foolish.'

'Not just any man.'

She saw a muscle tick in his jaw. 'I'm not the kind of man a woman like you needs.'

'I don't believe that. You were gentle and caring... And what do you mean *a woman like me?*'

'I'm not just talking physical needs here, Carissa. Emotional needs. Stability, commitment. The long haul. That's what a woman like you is looking for. And I'm not the man for that job.'

'Who says I'm looking for commitment? I just got over one disaster. I'm not looking to get myself another. I also think you underestimate yourself, Ben. Find the right woman and—'

'I'm not husband material, period. No woman should shackle herself to someone who killed a man.'

Oh, my God. Something shivered down her spine as an image of the dark, dangerous stranger she'd seen two evenings ago flashed before her eyes. But it wasn't fear. That man *couldn't* kill, she knew that. 'What happened?'

'I handed Rave the keys to my car. He was like a brother to me, and I killed him as sure as putting a bullet in his head.'

Carissa released the breath that had backed up in her throat. The grief she heard in his voice, the pain she saw in the grim twist of his lips, tore at her heart. But the news had reported excessive alcohol and speed had caused the accident. 'No. He made a choice.'

Ben rubbed his knuckles over his chin. 'A choice that was a direct consequence of *my* actions. If he'd had his way we'd have been halfway home by morning. I put my own needs above his, something a father or older brother would never do, and that's what I was to him.'

Even in the dimness Carissa could see the demons that haunted him, the shadowed eyes, the cool wash of moonlight over the tense line of his jaw.

'Tell me,' she prompted, sensing he'd not talked about it with anyone and was only now finding the nerve.

He looked up at the sky but he wasn't seeing it. He was back in Broken Hill. 'Rave wasn't in his room when I rang later that night. His mobile phone was off—a bad sign—he wanted Jess to be able to contact him at all times. I borrowed a car. Someone had seen him so I knew the direction he'd taken. Ten minutes later I saw the flames, smelled petrol, burning…' Silence filled the growing chasm between them. 'He hadn't been wearing the seat belt. I found him twenty metres farther on.'

Suddenly Carissa felt cold. She didn't want to hear any more.

'I tried to remember CPR. I wanted to bring him back…' His stone-edged voice cracked. 'His eyes were…'

'Ben. Don't blame yourself.' She shifted nearer, but, sensing he wouldn't welcome physical contact, she didn't touch him.

But she wanted to. Her natural instinct to offer the comfort of touch welled inside her. He looked so lost and vulnerable. His eyes were too bright, too shiny in the moon-glow when he looked out across the paddocks.

'It shows you the sort of friend I am, the sort of man I am.'

The sort that couldn't commit to someone, particularly someone like Carissa, he was trying to say, even though she'd already told him she wasn't ready for that at this point in her life. 'It's okay,' she said. 'I get the message loud and clear. I'm not looking for anything from you except the rent money.' But, oh, my…if she had the nerve…a wild, no-strings-attached affair… The very idea sent a wave of heat crashing through her body.

One corner of his mouth tipped up momentarily. As if he'd read her thoughts. Her totally inappropriate, ill-timed thoughts. 'Whatever you say.'

Oh, he wasn't helping. 'Any time you want to…*talk*…' She trailed off, noticing his focus had already turned inwards again.

'I'll be away for the next few days. Some business I've got to take care of in Melbourne. I'm not sure when I'll be back.'

A woman. She didn't know how she knew, but she did. Perhaps it was the subtle softening in his voice, the almost sad, faraway look in his eyes.

She pushed up and stood hugging her arms against the cool evening air. 'Your life's your own. You don't have to report in to me.'

But an uncomfortable new sensation burned within her. She couldn't get past it. The thought of that hot skin and hard muscle, his clever hands on some other woman, ignited something inside her that she'd never experienced. After all, Alasdair had never looked at other women.

Jealousy, plain and not-so-simple.

Something she'd better get used to fast.

CHAPTER FIVE

On Monday morning Carissa was too preoccupied to worry about her sexy lodger. She faced the unpleasant prospect of having George Christos throw her indiscretions in her face. Worse, much worse, there was no doubt in her mind she'd also be cleaning out her locker and collecting her final pay. Old Georgie was infamous for firing employees over the smallest infractions.

Ben had left before she'd risen and she hadn't seen him. She'd breathed a sigh of relief and told herself the less she saw of him, the better off she'd be.

She spotted George Christos by a potted palm on her way to his office and executed a quick ninety-degree turn. Damn. The last thing she wanted was a scene in the lobby.

'Ms Grace.' He puffed up to her. 'I tried to ring you at home but you'd already left.'

Squaring her shoulders, she turned. 'I thought we had a meeting—' she checked her watch '—in ten minutes.'

He mopped his brow with a stiff red handkerchief. 'I don't think that will be necessary. I've…ah…reconsidered.' He seemed to stumble on the word and his Adam's apple bobbed against his precisely knotted matching red tie. 'We all make mistakes and the Cove needs your expertise.' A pause. 'So we'll see you as usual on Friday evening?' He smiled, but it didn't quite reach his eyes.

She blinked in shocked amazement. 'You don't want to discuss it?'

He hesitated as if choosing his words, then said, 'I don't think that will be necessary. I'm sure it won't happen again.'

'Thank you, Mr Christos,' she said stiffly. Imagining yanking that tie and telling him right where to stick his job. Satisfying but out of the question.

Turning, she stalked away, heels tapping over the marble-tiled floor and, in defiance, exiting through the guest entrance rather than the employees' side door.

With an unanticipated free hour to kill, she headed for the Centrepoint shopping mall instead of the station. She stopped at a music shop, her attention drawn to the sign 'XLRock.' A trio of young males in leather and studs leered down at her from a poster on the wall. God. It was like looking inside someone's nightmare.

Beneath the poster she saw a book about the band. She flicked through the pages. Near the back was a small photograph of a long-haired Ben. She might have missed it but for the eyes—deep forest-green, soulful eyes.

But the sleeveless black leather vest over that bare chest... It threw her off course, making her shudder, yet shiver with a perverse thrill at the same time. She'd touched that chest, with her fingers, with her lips. Those nipples had brushed hers. And she was intimately acquainted with what hid beneath those tight leather pants. Whew. Her cheeks heated as she glanced furtively about her to make sure she was alone.

Dragging her gaze from the picture, she focused on the article. 'Ben Jamieson, financial backer for XLRock, is himself a passionate classical guitarist and composer... He's also written several tracks for XLRock, a departure from his usual style...'

Her breath caught in her lungs as amazement filled her. Classical guitarist and composer. Ben wasn't the man he wanted her to think he was. There was another side to Ben Jamieson that, for whatever reason, he'd not wanted to share with Carissa. Apparently he'd been a father-figure to Rave Elliot for the past fourteen years. And he said he didn't do long-term commitment. She shook her head at the contradiction.

Fifteen minutes later, Carissa stepped out into Sydney's bustle and the smells of pasta and pastries and exhaust fumes. Oppressive heat fought with blasts of cool from air-conditioned stores as she wended her way through the crowds to the station. But her mind was preoccupied with Ben. She'd read a list of his musical achievements, even recognised a couple of pieces he'd composed.

She stopped at the local supermarket on the way home. With no car she had to shop daily. When she arrived back at the house she found a package on the front step, which she balanced on top of the groceries as she pushed inside.

She dumped the groceries in the kitchen, then took the mystery parcel to her bedroom. She read the attached card first. 'An early birthday present. Enjoy. Love, Mel.'

Inside pink tissue paper Carissa found a skimpy, sexy, *see-through* white nightgown. She ran her fingers over the cool, smooth silk and lace. Just what was Mel thinking?

The answer was obvious and she couldn't resist turning to the mirror. As she shook the gown out a small packet fell to the floor. She didn't recognise what it was until she read the label: 'Lubricated for her comfort. Extra large.'

Oh... She felt the hot surge of remembered passion, saw the flush spring to her cheeks, and spun away from the incriminating reflection. With a stifled whimper, she snatched up the dangerous packet and stuffed it in the bottom of her underwear drawer.

She should never have told Mel about the virgin bit. But it was sweet of her to think of the gown. She rewrapped it in its tissue and slid it into the drawer with the condoms, out of harm's—and temptation's—way and hurried into the kitchen.

Did condoms have a use-by date? Carissa wondered as she stacked away the groceries. She shook her head at her own no-sex rule. It was a darn shame she wouldn't be seeing one of those condoms on display any time soon.

Ben stuffed the plush teddy he'd bought at the airport under his arm and walked up the path to the gracious apartment in one of Melbourne's trendy suburbs. If there was a time he'd wanted to be anywhere but the place he was standing right now, he couldn't remember it.

The woman who opened the door had flyaway brown hair tucked behind her ears. A sheer Indian-style dress skimmed ankles that jingled with tiny silver bells. The chubby baby on her hip ogled Ben open-mouthed, then tucked his head beneath his mother's chin. 'Ben.' Her face blanched as she backed up, grey eyes wide and sad. And angry.

He had to force his voice to work. 'Hello, Jess. Hey, Timmy.' He touched the boy's check, which was smeared with some sort of goo.

Her mouth compressed. 'I told you I'd let you know when I was ready to see you.'

'I couldn't stay away any longer, Jess.'

She blew a sharp breath through her nose. 'I guess you'd better come in, then.'

She turned and walked down an airy passage, feet padding on the parquetry floor. The aroma of fried food and stewed apples mingled with aged wood and polish as they neared the back of the house, and he stepped into a family area cluttered with toys. Dishes were stacked in the sink.

'I wasn't expecting company,' she said, removing a pile of folded nappies from an armchair to the table with one hand. She put Timmy in a playpen in the middle of the room.

'Here you go, champ.' Ben knelt down and set the teddy in front of the boy. Timmy watched him through Rave's black eyes and pain etched itself across the dark corners of Ben's heart. The kid would never remember his father.

'I'm not company, Jess.' He straightened and turned to her. 'Rave and I were family. *We're* family.'

'Is that so?' Her voice was chipped ice. 'Where were you, Ben, when my husband died? Was it gambling or a woman this time?'

Clenching his jaw, he took a step towards her, laid a hand on her shoulder. He would not allow her to think the worst of Ben Jamieson. That he reserved for himself. 'Jess, I'm sorry.' She remained unyielding as he folded himself around her, but he felt the tremors ripple through her too-thin body. 'Let go, I'm here. Please…'

'To ease your conscience, Ben?'

She pulled away. He closed his eyes briefly. He deserved that, and more.

Wet, racking sobs filled the silence. Timmy, sensing something was wrong, began to whimper. Jess pulled a tissue from her pocket, blew her nose, then picked up a training cup and gave it to her son. 'It's okay, baby, Mummy's okay.'

Ben watched her, light streaming blue and gold over her body through the old stained glass in the upper kitchen window, and thought how Rave would have loved to have seen her there.

Finally she looked at him. 'Tell me what happened. Don't pretty it up with what you think I want to hear. The truth, Ben.'

'Jess… It won't bring him back.'

'He was angry with you—I know because he rang me.'

'He wanted to come home. To you.'

'No, Ben, he wanted his own way. We both know how he was.'

Often egocentric, inclined to sulk. And on this gig he'd been more moody than usual. 'He was sober when I gave him the keys.'

'Of course he was. I know you wouldn't let him drink and drive.' She hugged her arms, knuckles white as she dug her fingers into her flesh. 'But you left him to do whatever it was you had to do—'

Guilt stabbed through Ben but he said, 'He was a grown man, Jess. He didn't need a babysitter. But you're right. I shouldn't've left him alone that night.'

'We'd had an argument the morning you left,' Jess said. 'A loud, ugly one. I never got the chance to say sorry.' Her soft grey eyes filled. Shaking her head, she crossed the floor and curled herself against his chest. 'It's not your fault, Ben. I know I've acted like it was, but that's grief. It's easier to blame someone else. I could have gone with him. I could've made the effort, paid someone to help with Timmy. But even if I'd been there he'd have done it his way. It always had to be his way.'

He held her close, noticing that unfamiliar baby smell on her clothes. 'I'd like to stay a couple of days, Jess, if you've got the room.'

'Of course I have the room—several spare rooms. We bought this house with four kids in mind.' She looked up and met his eyes, then touched his cheek. 'There'll always be a place here for you, Ben.'

'Thanks, Jess. Anything you need, anything at all, let me know.'

She had everything except what she wanted most. Once he'd almost envied what Rave and Jess had together. Now he was just plain grateful he'd never gotten involved with anyone.

Late in the afternoon Ben watched Carissa pedal down the drive and off to work. He'd thought by staying an extra few days in Melbourne to see Jess and his mother he'd have gotten over this need to see her. Nope. He couldn't take his eyes off the cute way her buttocks curved over that too-small seat.

He turned from the kitchen window and shook his head at the cold meat and salad she'd left. He was capable of feeding himself, but would she listen?

So he would put his evening to good use and see what needed doing outside since she couldn't afford to pay anyone. Feeling uncharacteristically domestic, he squirted a generous amount of lemon detergent and began rinsing the dishes she'd left in the sink. Mum always said that the dishes…

His hands stilled mid-swish. After he'd said goodbye to Jess he'd spent the better part of two days with his mother reminiscing about happier times. The same as he'd done last month, and the month before that.

Nothing changed.

He finished the dishes quickly. It would be more productive to put his mind to something he could make a difference to.

He was already outside when he heard the front door slam. He resented the way his heart shifted gears and his mood lifted at the thought of seeing her again so soon. But it didn't stop him retracing his steps.

He searched the house until he remembered he'd left the door open to catch the breeze. He stood in the family room and watched sunbeams dance over the piano's polished lid, and scraped at his jaw. His fingers itched but he shook his head. Leave the music to Carissa.

Then he remembered he wasn't supposed to be in here unless invited. As he turned to leave he saw the solitary birthday card. It was from Melanie and she'd written the date: twenty-seventh February. Today. He tapped it against his lips, then set it back. Apart from Melanie he hadn't seen anyone else round here who gave a damn.

He returned to his room to make a supper reservation for two.

Carissa slid the last drinks onto the table, searched in her apron for change. 'Thank you, sir.'

Nearly ten o'clock. The zipper on her only black skirt had broken and the safety pin was digging into her hip. Her feet ached and she still had to cycle home. Uphill, and the air was probably still warm and sticky outside.

The aroma of char-grilled meat and hot fat hung in the air. She thought of the scented bubble bath she was going to treat herself to, and, what the heck, she might even crack open that mini bottle of champagne left over from Christmas. She didn't care in which order she did them, so long as the water was hot, the bubbly cold. If she had to spend her birthday alone, at least she could do it in style.

'Carissa, go home.' Rosie, a plump, redheaded waitress pointed to the car park as Carissa pushed through the swing door to the kitchen. 'I'll finish here; you look beat.'

'Thanks, I think I will.'

She changed into shorts and left by the rear door to collect her bike. The air steamed with the scent of hot tar and vegetation. One dim light slicked a faint sheen over the few cars left.

Perspiration slid down her neck as she strapped her pack to her bike, then unlocked the chain. She didn't see the flicker of movement or hear the furtive scuff of feet until it was too late.

A man slid out of the shadows to her left and a rough hand clamped over her mouth. 'I've got a knife.' His voice scraped over her like rusty nails. To prove it, something sharp prodded her ribs. Her stomach spasmed in terror. The odour of beer and stale sweat almost suffocated her.

'See that car?' She tried to nod, but her head was held fast. 'You're going to move, nice and slow.'

A strangled noise bubbled up her throat. Panic spurted through her veins; her mind whirled. Her fingers tightened on the bike chain she still by some miracle held in her hand. She swung it behind her head, felt it connect, heard the whip and thud as it hit its target.

The sudden loosening of his hold and his strangled curse had her tottering backwards for a second before she swung around, primed to scream. Then she saw Ben. And screamed anyway.

'Are you all right?' She felt the energy of his anger beneath the quietly spoken words.

When her head nodded like a puppet, he leaned over the mugger's sprawled body. 'Ring the cops.'

The rear door slammed open and Brad, one of the cooks, ran out. 'Hey! Rosie, someone, ring the cops!' He came at a dead run, a hot fry-pan dripping grease in his hand.

'Carissa, oh, my God!' Rosie was down the steps and all over Carissa in a shot.

'I'm okay, it's okay.' But she heard the edge of hysteria in her voice. 'I…I have to ring the police.'

'Someone else'll do it,' Rosie said, leading her back to the restaurant. 'The guys can keep watch out here. Come inside and sit down.'

Carissa sank gratefully onto a chair while Rosie rushed off. She couldn't seem to draw air into her lungs.

'It's okay, sweetheart. Breathe slowly.' Ben's voice in her ear, calling her sweetheart, his arms around her.

Relaxing instantly, she felt her pulse returning to something approaching normal. Then he was on his haunches, holding her against him, his freshly showered scent so sweet and safe against her nose as he smoothed her hair.

'Cops'll want a statement,' he said. 'You up to it?'

She nodded and looked at him for the first time. His voice might have been controlled, but his eyes were dark with concern, his mouth a tight, thin line.

'Can you walk?'

'Yes.'

'We'll go outside where it's less crowded.'

'What are you doing here?'

'Coming to see you.' He hustled her out to the front of the restaurant as the sounds of sirens drew closer.

'Why?'

'Later.' He set her on the chair at one of the little wrought-iron tables, then started back inside. 'I'll get Rosie for you.'

A breeze cooled her sweaty skin. Her legs were smeared with grime and she really, really wanted a shower to wash away the lingering sensation of the scum's body on hers.

Twenty minutes passed before the excitement died down. Rosie sat with her while she talked to the police, then she caught sight of Ben's car as it exited the car park and pulled up in front.

'He's your lodger?' Rosie said as he stepped out and rounded the hood.

'Yeah.' Grimly gorgeous in what had been a white T-shirt, and freshly pressed khaki trousers, he looked as if he'd been on his way to a night on the town.

'Had him long?'

'Couple of weeks.' Carissa couldn't help the weak laugh. 'You make him sound like some kind of condition.'

'Hey, in the interests of medical science, I'd suffer him gladly.' He stood by the car, hands in his pockets. 'I think he's waiting for you.'

Carissa's heart bumped at the idea. She smoothed clammy hands over the front of her thighs and rose. 'Thanks, Rosie.'

Ben stepped forward as Carissa approached. 'I'm taking you home.'

'My bike...'

'We'll get it tomorrow.' He opened the passenger door.

As she hauled her aching backside onto the seat she was greeted with the smell of old vinyl and roses. Ben reached behind her to the back seat, then laid a bunch of yellow roses on her lap. 'Happy birthday.'

'Oh...' She met his eyes and fought a sudden fierce desire to cry.

'You leave this lot behind and I'll develop serious feelings of inadequacy.'

'Thank you. How did you know it was my birthday?' But he'd already shut her door.

'I'm driving you to work from now on,' he told her as he slid inside, swung a U-turn and headed home.

The no-negotiation statement startled her. 'No.'

'What do you mean, no? You were attacked, for God's sake,

anything could have happened—why did you put your bicycle in such an exposed place?'

'I'll put it somewhere else. It wouldn't have made a difference if I'd driven or cycled, the risk's the same.'

'Not if I'm there. Listen up, Carissa, while I'm here I'll be driving you and I don't intend discussing it.'

'Fine.' She crossed her arms. 'Let's not discuss it.'

'Fine.' He shoved the gear stick through its paces.

She looked away, out the window. 'I can take care of myself.' But, oh, it felt nice to have someone watching out for her. She'd been independent for so long, she'd forgotten there was any other way. But it would only make it harder when he left.

'Thought you said you weren't going to discuss it.'

'Discuss what?' she said, and drew the scent of roses to her nose.

Two minutes later Ben pulled into the drive. He could barely contain his fury. The image of that low-life with his hands on Carissa burned into his brain. Every time he thought about what might have happened if he'd been a few seconds later…

'If you hadn't turned up you wouldn't even have known,' she murmured.

'Is it women in general or just you?' He slammed his hands on the nearest available surface—the steering wheel.

'Meaning?'

'Do you always have to have the last word?'

'It's hard not to when you live alone.'

'You don't live alone. For now.' He pushed out of the car as the pale moon slid behind a shifting cloud. The sounds of night drifted through the air, the distant rumble of waves breaking on the beach, a nightjar's hoot.

He rounded the hood, but Carissa was already marching towards the steps, back stiff, shoulders squared. He followed a few steps behind. She'd cope with whatever life tossed her way, including him, he knew. But that cowardly bastard tonight had put a serious dent in her self-assurance.

In the kitchen he leaned against the sink as he watched her take a vase from the cupboard, fill it with water and arrange her roses. She was making an effort to appear unfazed, but he knew better. Her face was china-white and fragile, her fingers not quite steady, her eyes dark, and right now avoiding his.

He hesitated a beat, then laid a hand on her shoulder. He felt her flinch, but she didn't shake him off. 'Go take a shower or a soak in the tub. You'll feel better for it. I'll still be here when you're done. I'll brew coffee.'

He felt her loosen beneath his fingers. 'Okay. Thanks. And thanks again for the flowers.'

Then she turned and looked at him and something unfamiliar settled in his chest. Because he didn't know what to do with the feeling he shrugged, stepped away. 'Hey, what are friends for?'

She left him standing there with the sensation that he'd somehow been sucked out of his depth.

He brewed the promised coffee, then took a wander around the house. Someone with Carissa's talent shouldn't be working in a dump like that. And if he hadn't been there, if he hadn't known it was her birthday... But he had, and he had to be content with that.

Thirty minutes later she entered the kitchen wrapped in an amethyst silk robe, her hair damp and piled on top of her head and smelling like flowers.

She rubbed at her arms. 'Thanks for your support tonight.'

'No worries. Just glad I was there.' He pushed up and moved to the coffee-maker. 'Feeling better?'

She rolled her shoulders, an unconscious movement, then stopped when she saw him watching. 'I'm fine.'

She didn't have a clue what a sight she made, tall and slim, like a lone fresh-picked iris.

She got to him. As he continued to watch her, deep down where he'd buried his vulnerability, he felt something stir. And he didn't like it, didn't want it.

Didn't need it.

They'd shared one night and she'd made it clear that was all she wanted. All he wanted. He wasn't looking for permanence; she wasn't his type.

But... He reached for her arm; his hand closed around firm flesh beneath smooth silk. Her breath jerked and he saw her swallow. There were marks on her neck, he noted grimly. 'It's okay,' he murmured. He wanted to reassure her, not frighten her. He wanted to make her forget the past couple of hours and just *be* with her.

'I told you I'm—'

'Fine. I know. Relax a minute.' He eased her onto a kitchen stool, then moved behind her and let his hands rest on her shoulders. When she didn't pull away, he slid his fingers beneath the edge of the silk. Slowly and gently dragged it out of the way, exposing her spine and the delicate lines of her collar-bones.

He slid his thumbs up either side of her spine and was rewarded with a sigh. Her skin was creamy smooth and fragrant, but the muscles beneath remained knotted and tense. He kneaded for several minutes in a silence broken only by the breeze whispering through the window and the night sounds beyond.

'Heard you playing Gershwin this morning,' he said, keeping his voice casual. '"Summertime," if I remember correctly.'

'One of my favourites. Did you grow up with music?'

'My father only allowed classical music in the house.' His hands tightened and he had to make a conscious effort not to press too hard.

'And your mother?'

'Had no say in it.'

'Your dad's the reason you don't like classical.'

He was the reason for a lot of bad things. How had the conversation circled to the unpleasant topic of his father?

'But you learnt guitar,' she prompted.

'When I was ten a mate's mum taught me in exchange for doing odd jobs around her garden. I used to practise with her old guitar in the shed when Dad was at work.' He no longer trusted his hands not to betray the dark emotions the memories had dragged up and dropped them to his sides. 'That'll do for now.'

'Thanks.' Rising, she shrugged back into her robe. 'You're a kind man, Ben Jamieson.'

Against his better judgement he let his eyes drop to her mouth, full, untinted and, right now, irresistibly tempting.

'Maybe you'll change your mind about that judgement,' he murmured, and, leaning in, he laid his lips on hers.

The instant jolt of heat, of lust, was expected; the tenderness he felt for her was not. The scent from her bath, subtle, cool and alluring, surrounded him until he thought he might drown in it. He thought he heard music, soft, haunting piano, but it was probably the night breeze stirring the wooden wind chimes outside.

He wanted to slide his hands lower, over that silk, feel her heat beneath the cool, but kept them stubbornly on her shoulders. She needed a friend tonight, nothing more.

With an effort he pulled back. He caught the dreamy light in her eyes before she masked it with something resembling indifference, although he sensed she was far from unaffected.

'You were on your way out tonight and I ruined your plans.' Her voice was husky as she brushed at the dirt-smeared T-shirt. 'That makes you a kind man.'

The touch of her fingers reminded him of how they'd felt on his bare skin. The thought of her touching him again in other places... He turned away to hide the hard evidence. 'It was nothing important.' She was better off not knowing. They were both better off. 'Good night.'

He headed for his room before she could reply.

CHAPTER SIX

CARISSA shot up in bed, heart pounding. Something had woken her. She heard it again, a shuffling outside her window. Her saliva dried in her throat. What if the low-life who'd tried to attack her the other night knew where she lived and had come to collect? She shook her head. Of course not; the police had him now.

Throwing back the sheet, she crept to the window. In the streetlight's dim glow a man was hunched on the verandah, head buried in his hands.

Ben. She watched his big frame heave and her throat constricted. What demons haunted him? Whatever they were, he kept it to himself. He needed a friend; he had no one right now. Except her.

Yet he'd shown her a tenderness she'd not expected. Nor would he knowingly display a hint of the open grief she was witnessing now. He slammed a fist against his thigh and her hand crept to her throat. She couldn't go to him—his pride would suffer if he knew she'd caught him at such an unguarded moment. But she wanted to.

Oh, hell. The timing was all wrong. She didn't want a relationship right now. She'd never know if it was the 'classic' rebound he told her it was. It could never be more than sexual attraction between them. He was wealthy, worldly and she was totally out of his league. The spark was there but that was all it was. All she'd let it be.

But there was something she could do. She could help him feel valued and useful, things she knew were lacking in his life right now. So she could let him help her—up to a point.

'Damn!' Carissa glared at the inch of murky dishwater in the sink. So not what she needed after a long day. She dragged the toolbox from its shelf and dumped it on the floor with a clatter.

'Problem?' Ben poked his head around the door. She hadn't seen him all day but he looked gorgeous and thoroughly beddable.

'I was getting a glass of water and the bloody sink's blocked again,' she muttered, sorting through the tools, trying not to think about Ben and bed at the same time.

When she looked around again, he was in the middle of the kitchen wearing only a pair of white hip-hugging briefs scrunched at one side as if he'd pulled them on in a hurry. And Lycra, for heaven's sake—didn't he realise it outlined every shadow, every masculine bump? Made every female cell in her body jump to attention?

She raised her eyes to his. He was watching her watching him. Of course he knew.

Dismissing the view with a silent snarl, she opened the cupboard door below the sink. Then she remembered she was going to give him the odd jobs to keep him occupied. 'Would you mind, Ben? I'm—' she spotted her hand and body lotion '—just going to give myself a hand massage.'

A smoky heat flickered in his eyes at the erotic image she'd unwittingly conjured as he leaned one tanned arm on the sink. *Much too close.* So close she could smell the warm, sleepy scent of his body.

She took a hasty step back. 'You just need to unscrew that U-shaped bit and—'

'I know.' All masculine know-how, he picked up the wrench dropped to his haunches and inspected the plumbing while Carissa stood back in her nightshirt and played the role of helpless female.

He muttered something to himself about plumbers, then turned, lay down on his back and wiggled himself into position under the pipe. The sight of that bronzed skin and finely honed torso taking up all the space on her kitchen floor snapped through her blood. The overhead light sheened the hard planes of muscle in his calves and thighs and...

And she needed to look somewhere else. Needed to *be* somewhere else—

She heard the sound of metal chiming on metal followed by, 'Grab the buck—' then the splash of water and a disgusted, 'Never mind.'

'Are you okay?' She dropped to her knees, then all fours when the only response was a muttered oath.

'Just wet.' He wriggled back out. Water glistened on the smooth line of his brow, in the grooves that bracketed his mouth. Her eyes followed a single drop as it slid over the faint stubble on his jaw into the hollow at his shoulder and onto the floor. Then their gazes caught, and in that sultry beat of heat she saw the water, the two of them, opportunity...

Déjà vu.

Heat pumped through her veins and ribbon-danced in her belly. She scrambled up, swiped up the tea-towel and thrust it at him. 'I'll leave you to it. Let me know when you're done,' she said, grabbing the bottle of lotion, backing away and escaping into the living room.

Good Lord. Collapsing onto the couch, she blew out a breath, squeezed her eyes shut. It didn't help. All she could see was Ben's semi-naked body as she made her escape. His semi-naked *aroused* body. Oh, she hadn't missed that not-so-tiny detail.

She unscrewed her bottle, poured lotion onto her hand and set the bottle back down with a firm 'chink.' The cream's smooth texture as she massaged her skin only fuelled her sensory overload. If she'd really wanted to escape she'd have gone to her bedroom. A traitor to herself. On the other hand she felt duty-bound to stick around until he finished, thank him politely and say good night.

She suddenly became aware that the clanging had stopped and heard his shower running. Now she had no choice but to wait and think about that big body slippery with water. Five minutes later he appeared at the doorway. His chest and its sprinkling of dark hair gleamed with damp under the old chandelier. Not that she was looking at his chest. Or the silky black boxer shorts he'd changed into.

'All fixed. For now.' Smelling of soap and clean man, he sat down beside her and squirted a dollop of her hand lotion onto his palms.

'Thanks.' She didn't know what else to say. It was nearly midnight, the job was done and she'd thanked him—she should go to bed. Instead, she rubbed in more cream. More heat.

The moment stretched on and on, thick with the scent of sweet ripe peaches and Ben. And temptation. Her body was already anticipating his touch. Her pulse was playing a fast "Minute Waltz" and a line of sweat prickled her spine. But she knew nothing would happen unless she wanted it to, unless she gave permission. She had that small control at least.

'Give me your hand.' His husky gravel voice scraped away any thought she'd had of being in control. In his eyes she saw a mutual acknowledgement they both understood. Lust, she assured herself. Nothing more.

She watched his hard, blunt fingers envelop her slim fair ones. His thumb drew a lazy circle in the centre of her palm, a slow, slippery massage that sent hot-cold shivers up her arm and through her veins. He raised their joined hands to eye-level, sliding his fingers against hers, liquid silk to liquid silk.

His eyes turned molten and sparked with green fire as she joined in the dance, sliding her slick fingers over his wrist, feeling the pulse that beat thick and strong and steady.

He pressed their joined hands to his lips. 'My room or yours? Or does the no-sex rule still stand?'

She felt his warm breath on her skin, the fullness of his lower lip against her thumb as he spoke. And totally melted. Why should she fight it? One night with Ben Jamieson wasn't enough. Why not take what he was obviously offering? What she wanted.

'No rules. My room.' She stood, amazed at the smooth way she'd said it when the word seemed to come from somewhere outside her body.

But he didn't release her hand. 'Are you sure?'

'It's only sex, right?'

She thought he looked momentarily taken aback, his eyes a mix of desire and bemusement. 'Is that what you want?'

He was almost at eye-level, lip-level. She leaned closer, touched her burning mouth to his. The spark smouldered, caught, sizzled. More sparks as he took a leisurely journey over her lips, then a long slow burn as his tongue slid inside and tangled with hers.

It was electric, carnal. Physical.

His breath hissed out. 'I need—'

'I have what you need,' she said against his mouth.

'I know you do, sweetheart, but I still need—'

'I have a whole box,' she said, tugging their joined hands, and watched surprise and arousal sharpen his eyes.

When they reached her room, she opened her drawer and placed the box on the quilt.

His eyes slid from the box to her. 'You're full of surprises tonight,' he said in that gravelly voice from the opposite side of the bed.

'It was a gift. From a responsible friend,' she added when he didn't reply. He just kept looking at her with hot eyes, as if visualising her without the nightshirt. Carissa reached for the hem of her nightshirt, drew it over her head and tossed it down. Cool air and hot eyes kissed her nipples. 'Your turn,' she said.

She kept her eyes on his as he pushed down his shorts, but she couldn't resist a downward glance. Flames licked at her belly. Oh, sweet heaven—and it would be. She swallowed. There was just so much of him. She hadn't seen him like this the last time. Big and bold and beautiful. And naked.

Drawing in a steadying breath, she shimmied out of her panties.

Cellophane crinkled as he slid the wrapper off and opened the box. 'Extra large,' she said, her eyes sliding over the fierce jut of his erection again. Was that sultry female voice hers?

A corner of his mouth kicked up. 'I noticed. You want to do the honours?' She shook her head once. 'I don't know how.' Unlike his other lovers, she thought. Another strike against her. But he didn't seem disappointed. Far from it. He smiled his crooked smile, that wicked smile that had no doubt seduced more than its fair share of the female population, and said, 'I'll teach you.'

He scooted around to her side of the bed, grasped her hand and clamped it around him. She felt the leashed power and stroked up, then down, testing, exploring, revelling in her discovery.

'Easy, sweetheart,' he muttered on a breathy exhalation. 'Here…' His hand closed over hers as he helped her roll the smooth latex down his hot, hard length. 'Simple.' The rasp in his voice stroked over her senses like serrated velvet.

She sighed out a trembling laugh. 'Yeah.' Not so simple was the rush of emotion that accompanied this intimacy, this developing bond, the need to be with him in this way.

Drawing back the covers, she lay down. The night beyond the open window was still and redolent with summer. The only sound she heard was her breathing as she struggled to draw oxygen into her lungs.

For a long time Ben didn't move. His dark, passion-filled eyes devoured her body. 'I've been dreaming about you like this. But the real thing is so much more. You're perfect. Almost too beautiful to touch.'

Impossibly turned on by his gaze and his admission that he'd dreamed of her—naked—she managed a smile. 'That would be a big disappointment.'

'For both of us,' he said and stretched out beside her.

The caress of his mouth on hers was a sweet prelude to more. He stroked her body as if he touched the most fragile china—her ear, throat, breasts, navel. Too gentle, too reverent to be pure lust.

Something like panic swamped her. She couldn't risk her heart to a man who'd be out of her life in weeks. Someone who was used to experienced lovers. She reached out and turned off the bedside lamp to avoid his eyes, to hide hers. The streetlight cast a silver light over them and Ben slid his hard, hair-roughened body over hers.

She knew that come morning she'd be alone with only his scent to mingle with hers on the linen. That was okay. That was right. But for now… Shifting so that his silky tip slid along her moisture-drenched flesh, she arched her hips.

Then he was inside her, the cool sheets a stunning contrast to his heat, the scents of peaches and male filling her nose, the soft sibilance of skin on skin.

Only sex, she chanted to herself as she rode the dizzying spiral towards climax. *Lust.* But the tiny voice sounded far, far away and unconvincing.

This wasn't lust. This was something way more dangerous.

Carissa adjusted the air-con so it blew on her face as they slid out of the drive in Ben's shiny new black Porsche. And it wasn't doing her any favours. When he left, she'd be back where she'd started: on her push bike. But, oh, the seats were butter-soft, and it smelled so rich and extravagant.

'Don't you have anything better to do than take me grocery shopping?' she said. 'Like a drive in the countryside to put this new toy through its paces?'

'We'll get round to it.'

She didn't argue, but the way he linked them into the future did strange things to her already-queasy stomach.

'You said I could cook tonight,' he continued. 'I want to select the ingredients myself.'

'You cooked last night.' And the night before that. It was becoming a habit. She told herself it was therapeutic for him, but what about her? Enough was enough. The man was insinuating his way into her life. Heck, he was charging his way in like a lifeguard into surf at Bondi Beach.

'As a matter of fact, I do have something to do this morning,' he said. 'I'm going to pick up those supplies I ordered for the porch steps.'

'I told you it's not your problem.' He'd already sanded some of the woodwork, but she'd not told him what colour trim she wanted because she knew he'd go right out and buy it. He'd fixed the leak on the roof and planed the kitchen door so it shut properly.

'Honestly… Couldn't you go compose a few songs?'

'No.' She felt a mental door slam in her face at the mention of his songwriting.

'Okay, there's a skydiving school not far away.'

The tension cleared a little and he cast her an *almost* grin. 'Only if you promise to come with me.'

'Jump out of a plane? Just the thought's enough to turn my stomach…' The queasiness rolled up and over, then passed, but left her feeling clammy and weak. *Not now, please.* She simply could not afford to take time off.

By the time they reached the supermarket she was almost feeling herself again. Because it seemed too much like a couple thing to let him push the trolley, she strode ahead and took one first, then set a brisk pace, pulling items off shelves in a race to stay one aisle ahead of him.

'Slow down, you'll have a heart attack,' Ben murmured, offloading a selection of red peppers, mushrooms and beans. He looked closer. 'Come to think of it, you look a little off colour again today. Not sleeping well?'

He could ask that question? 'I slept fine,' she lied, and turned away from his probing eyes. 'Don't look at me like that. I've made a doctor's appointment for tomorrow afternoon, so drop it.' Distracted, she vacillated between China Pekoe and Earl Grey tea, then popped English Breakfast in the trolley. 'I need…jam setter,' she improvised.

'You make jam?'

'Not without jam setter, I don't.'

'I didn't know you were that domesticated. I thought those skills died in the sixties.'

'There's a lot you don't know about me, Ben Jamieson.'

For a moment his eyes challenged hers. Then he hooked his thumbs in the front of his jeans. 'What is it and where do I find it?'

She smiled at him. 'I'm not sure. Go look for me?' She watched his gorgeous jeans-clad backside as he strode off on his quest. Then she shook her head. What was she thinking? She couldn't afford to let her mind stray to forbidden territory.

But did he have to be so…nice? So attractive? So…everything. He'd be off in a few weeks. Maybe even days. Who knew? No point in getting used to having him around. Would he return to his music? Would he stay in Australia or head overseas? A man like him was always on the move, never settling in one place—he'd told her as much that first night. She wanted a home and family one day.

'Seek and ye shall find.'

She blinked as Ben tossed the requested packet into the trolley. 'Huh? Oh. Right.' Distracted, she pushed the trolley towards the checkout. Pulling out her purse, she laid cash on the counter before Ben could flip out one of his flashy platinum credit cards.

As the mall's glass doors slid open letting in a blast of hot air she almost gagged. Her knees turned wobbly; the sour taste of vomit climbed up her throat. She did *not* want Ben witnessing this. It would pass.

Gritting her teeth, she said, 'I want to browse the mall a while. I'll walk home when I'm through.' Abandoning Ben and the trolley, she walked casually until she lost herself in the crowd, then fled to the ladies' room.

* * *

'According to the date of your last period, you're seven weeks pregnant, Carissa. Which explains why you haven't been feeling well.'

Dr Beaton had been the family doctor for years, had treated her childhood illnesses and now…now he was telling her she was pregnant.

'But that's impossible. I can't be…' He slid his bifocals down his nose. 'Not *seven* weeks. I mean… we only did it once…that night…he used a condom.' Her cheeks felt like fire and she could barely get the words past her throat. Of course she knew sometimes it only took once. And did that make her any less pregnant?

'Condoms have a higher failure rate than people often believe.' She sagged against the chair. 'Are you sure?'

'Carissa.' His voice softened. 'Perhaps you'd feel more comfortable discussing your options with my colleague. I'm referring all my obstetrics patients on now; I'm getting too old.' He smiled at her over his glasses, then scribbled something on a pad, tore it off and handed it to her. 'Dr Elise Sharman's a gynaecologist and obstetrician. If you like I'll ask Jodie to arrange for an appointment for you.'

'Thank you.' Her entire body felt numb. With those few words her life had just been turned upside down.

'Do you have an ongoing relationship with the baby's father?' She shook her head. 'Is there anyone you can talk to? Melanie…? I can arrange for a social worker…'

His words seemed to be coming from a distance. As if in a dream she nodded as she listened to his advice about health care, heard him tell her Jodie would ring her when she'd made the appointment with Dr Sharman.

Nothing seemed real. She stepped from the cool surgery and out into the heavy afternoon heat. The oyster-coloured sky was thickening. A car spewed hot exhaust as it pulled away from the kerb, its fumes smoking on the still air. A couple of kids yelled as they sped by on skateboards, nearly knocking her down. It occurred to her as absurd that in a few years' time it could be her child hurtling down the footpath.

Hers and Ben Jamieson's.

Where would he be by then?

She'd promised to call when she'd finished at the surgery but she wasn't ready to face him. Not yet. Not until she'd thought through all possible scenarios and decided what to do. And for that she needed Gran.

Half an hour later, she sat in the cemetery under the old casuarinas. 'Gran, I've got myself into what you'd have called "the family way".' She unscrewed the bottle of water she'd purchased at a deli along the way, took a mouthful, then dribbled a few cool drops from the bottle between her breasts.

Her hand skimmed her flat stomach, and wonder struck her. Family. She'd never be alone again. No matter how often she'd told herself that was how she'd wanted it, the knowledge that a new life was growing inside her, a part of her, filled her with awe and a sense of connection.

'A one-night stand, Gran.' She lifted her face as the first drops of rain pinged the ground. The damp, dusty scent mingled with the heat. 'A man doesn't get himself into this predicament. So much for equality of the sexes, huh?'

She reached out to the headstone and closed her eyes. 'If you were here, what would you have said to me now?'

The words came to her on a tide of love. She'd never questioned where they came from, nor did she doubt their wisdom. She simply knew, and accepted.

Everything happens for a reason.

'If only I knew what that reason was. He doesn't want commitment.' Her gaze slid to the old trees that had stood since long before her grandmother had been laid to rest, their roots firmly in the ground. Not Ben's. 'He doesn't even want to stay in one place. Darn sure he doesn't want a child.'

Sweat and rain ran in rivulets down her face, her T-shirt clung to her back in the saunalike air. 'He's filthy rich and I'm scraping the bottom of my bank account. What if he thinks I want his money, that I trapped him into this? If he stays much longer he's going to see my pregnancy whether I tell him or not. I don't think he's the type to walk away from responsibility. He'd feel obligated. Obligation would turn to resentment.'

She thought of the lingering glances she'd become increasingly aware of, the way her heart leapt when she caught him watching, the way he turned away when she did.

'When he leaves it's going to hurt.' And he would leave— she'd make sure of it, for her own sanity, and his. 'He doesn't need me, or our baby. Ben Jamieson needs something in his life, but it's not us.'

In a defensive move she suddenly became aware of, she crossed her arms in front of her. She would protect herself and the child inside her with everything she had, that much she knew. She could take another lodger, take on some piano students in her home—if she still had a home.

Her thoughts circled back to Ben. How could she *not* tell him? A man had a right to know. What he did with the information was up to him. But not yet. When she had everything in place, she'd contact him, wherever he might be by then.

CHAPTER SEVEN

BEN eased the cumbersome plank into place and reached for the pack of nails. At least now Carissa could reach her front door without fear of falling through the steps.

He stopped a moment, caught in the past. The smell of fresh-sawed wood and Mum's roast lamb, the sound of hammering as he and his father worked together to put in kitchen shelving.

It should have been a team effort, father and son. His father had grudgingly agreed to let him help, and Ben was bursting with eight-year-old pride.

But the shelving was too heavy for a kid's scrawny arms to hold and somehow the end slipped out of his hands. The young Ben had let the team down. Again. He backed away from the red-hot anger in his father's eyes.

'Damn boy'll never be good at anything,' he muttered.

The child's self-worth took another dive.

'Get lost, kid. That's what you do best, isn't it? You hit a problem, you're gone.'

The past is past. Ben pulled out nails, hammered, pulled nails, hammered. Those hands his father the cop had scorned had learned how to lift a man's wallet in defiance, had learned how to make a guitar sing, bring pleasure to a woman.

He'd died before Ben could show him he wasn't the failure his father had told him he was. 'Wherever you are,

Dad, this one's for you.' He drove the last nail in, threw the hammer down.

But there was a grain of truth in his father's words. He thought of Rave. Ben had let that team down too. He'd tossed in his song-writing, packed away his guitar. *Hit a problem and you're gone.*

Enough. Pushing the memories away, he moved back to look at the finished steps, vaguely annoyed that he'd have to put off the staining until the weather looked more promising. Then he gazed up at the roof trim, sanded and ready to paint. What would it be like to belong somewhere? To belong to someone, to share their life?

Carissa. What would it be like to come home to her every night? *Get that thought right out of your idiot head.*

It started to rain. He glanced at his watch. Carissa should have finished at the doctor's by now. Perhaps he should go over and check, but she wouldn't thank him for tracking her movements. They didn't keep tabs on each other. She'd ask for a lift if she needed one.

He collected the tools, then headed round the back to store them away. Inside he found himself drawn to the living room once more. The stained ivory keys reflected the sombre light from the window.

Perhaps he could play again after all. Not guitar, but piano. Carissa's piano. Touching the keys she touched, making the music she made. He raised the lid, picked out a few keys, noting the slightly out-of-tune E flat.

The click and scrape at the front door warned him Carissa was home. He watched her come in. She didn't see him immediately and slumped back against the door and closed her eyes. Rain dewed her skin and hair and an aura of fragility surrounded her.

He knew better, but he wanted to reach out, run his hands over those drooping shoulders, draw her close and protect her from whatever was bothering her. Unease slid through him. Had the doctor given her bad news?

Because he knew she hated looking to others for support, particularly him, he stayed where he was. 'Why didn't you ring, Miz Independence?' His voice was gruffer than he'd intended.

Her eyes flew open and she pushed away from the door as if she were on springs. 'What are you doing in here?'

'Piano needs tuning.'

'I know. You startled me. I'm not used to people lurking around the house.'

'Sorry. What did the doc say?' he asked, following her to the kitchen. He watched her open the fridge, pull out a carton of juice.

Ignoring his question, she lifted it in his direction. 'Want one?'

'Thanks.'

She poured two glasses, put his on the table and drank hers at the bench. Not once did she glance his way.

He waited for a reply and was deciding she'd gone conveniently deaf when she said, 'I need to take more calcium.'

'Okay.' He reached for his glass. 'Now tell me what's really bothering you.'

'I don't want to talk about it.'

He noted an underlying edge to her tone, and knew when a woman made up her mind not to talk about something it was pointless to pursue it. Still, he had to ask, 'You sure?'

Her shoulders stiffened, but still she didn't face him. 'If you really want to know, you're bothering me. Now, if you're through, I'm going to cool off in the shower before I get tea ready.'

Temper simmered but he tamped it down. 'I don't want you fixing my meals, Carissa. You've got six hours on your feet coming up.'

'It's called a job. It's what most of us do.' She finished her juice, rinsed her glass and upturned it on the sink. 'I'm going to take that shower.'

He waited till she'd left, then took two eggs from the fridge to make himself an omelette. Damned if she was going to cook for him. The frying-pan clanged as he dumped it on the stove.

Damned if he was going to feel responsible for whatever her problem was.

The sound of the shower had his stomach clenching, and it had nothing to do with her state of mind and everything to do with her current state of undress. Heat rushed through his loins at the image that gentle splashing invoked. Her fingers slick with soap sliding over creamy flesh, dusky nipples puckering under the spray, rivulets of water running down her back between the tempting curves of her buttocks.

But she'd looked pale beneath that delicate summer tan. Tense. Vulnerable.

He slammed a hand onto the bench. And damned if he was going to let her get to him.

Some hours later, Ben set the platter of paté and cheese on the table. He lit the scented candle he'd found and stuck in a bottle, then turned off the overhead light.

'You shouldn't have.' Carissa's tone gave no hint of how she felt about his midnight supper. A lingering scent of fried onions clung to her work clothes.

He dropped the lighter on the table. 'Probably not.'

'Ben?' Clear and direct eyes met his. 'About this afternoon; I'm sorry if I was rude. Correction—I *was* rude, and I apologise.'

He smiled, relieved to have the air a little clearer between them. 'And I shouldn't have pushed. Relax, you're tired. Have a bite to eat and I'll let you get to bed.'

'Ben, we need to talk.' She sat down, resting her forearms on the table.

Her hair was still tied back, loose tendrils floating at her temples. He wanted to undo the tortoiseshell clasp and watch that pale gold silk tumble down and soften her face.

'Not tonight,' he murmured, and watched the way her eyes reflected the candlelight. 'Let's just sit here a moment and unwind.'

He spread paté on a cracker and held it out. 'Try this. It's from the gourmet shop on the corner.'

'Thank you.' She took it from his fingers, avoiding contact, took a tiny nibble and set it down.

Was he imagining it or was she more than tired? She'd been uncommunicative on the short drive from work. He knew he shouldn't, but he wanted to know what was going on in that complex head of hers.

Hadn't he told himself he didn't want to get involved? But he'd never quite decided. A surprise, since he'd always known his own mind. Carissa had the ability to throw him off-track. 'Try the cheese if you're calcium-deficient. New Zealand gouda.'

But she shook her head. 'I've got something I need to say and I have to say it tonight.' She seemed to take a fortifying breath and placed both palms on the table. 'I have to renege on our rental agreement.'

Something in her tone told him whatever the reason was, she wasn't going to let him in on it, but he set his plate aside, his appetite killed. 'Mind telling me why?'

He saw the flicker in her eyes, the way her gaze didn't meet his when she said, 'I'm used to doing things for myself, on my own. Now I turn around and you're there—rescuing me, chauffeuring me, cooking, renovating my house.' She waved a hand. 'I don't want to depend on anyone. You're not here forever, and the longer you stay, the more I'll take for granted. It'll make it harder in the long term.'

'That's rubbish, Carissa. It's more than that and we both know it. You gave up your solitary existence when you took in a lodger.'

'You're more than—'

Her quick indrawn breath told him she'd said more than she'd intended.

'Yeah,' he said softly. Shifting closer, he cupped her jaw 'Your lover. Your only lover.'

He didn't miss the flash of emotion in her eyes, her tiny

shudder under his hand as the air charged with the heat of that encounter. The attraction was still there—on both sides—simmering beneath the impassive expression she'd reverted to. 'Forget the rental agreement,' he murmured, and leaned in.

She sat utterly still as he skimmed his lips over hers. A breeze drifted through the room as if someone had sighed, setting the candle's flame wavering and bringing its jasmine scent closer.

His hand slid lower, and he felt the pulse in her neck leap beneath his fingers. Taking his time, he probed deeper, running his tongue over her lips until she opened for him, till he felt her jaw soften, her resistance melt.

He could change her mind about the rental agreement. He couldn't seem to come up with one solid reason why he should, except that for the first time in a long time he was content here in her home.

One slim-fingered hand rose over his forearm and crept up his chest. He felt the slight tremble in her touch and shifted nearer. He remembered the night he'd made more than her hand tremble. Her whole body had vibrated beneath his.

He wanted that feeling again. Now, now when he knew her better, he wanted something more than a sweaty bout between the sheets. The twinge of conscience that he'd taken that innocence without thought, without the care it had deserved, even if she had begged for it, had him gentling his movements.

He focused his senses on the moment. On the soft, sweet tasting skin beneath his lips as he mated his tongue to hers, her unique feminine scent, the candlelight that flickered over her closed eyelids.

He'd never been a man given to romance, but Carissa seemed to draw it from him. The beginnings of a song hummed through his head, something slow and dreamy and he hoped he could remember it later and commit it to paper.

But he felt her stiffen, saw regret in her eyes as she pulled back. 'I shouldn't have let it get so complicated,' she whispered.

He touched her cheek. 'It doesn't have to be complicated. I don't mind helping out. I need something to focus on right now. You're doing *me* a favour.' She shook her head, and the tensed muscles he hadn't noticed tightened in his gut.

'No,' she said. 'I want to be alone and I can't be with you here. You…you're in my face, Ben.'

In her face. And right now that face was a mask. He didn't buy it. Not for a second.

He had no choice.

He stared at her for a long moment, wondering why it hurt so much for a man who didn't want to get involved. Then he pushed up. 'I guess that's my cue to exit.'

'I only meant…' She chewed on her lip, and to his surprise her eyes filled with moisture. She blinked it away. 'Another month's probably okay.'

Anger warred with impatience. Anger that he felt the tug of regret at leaving and impatience to be gone. 'I don't think so. I'll be out before noon tomorrow.'

'You will keep in contact, won't you? I…' She twisted her fingers together, as if she actually *cared* that she was kicking him out.

Was that the action of a logical person? 'You're one confused woman, you know that?'

'I want to know you're okay. Is that a crime?'

He saw her desperation and wanted, inexplicably, to reach for her, so he stepped back, putting the table between them, a barrier for his emotions. 'You want to worry about someone, worry about yourself.'

She flinched as if he'd slapped her. Her lips still glistened from their kiss, her hair was coming adrift from its clasp, and her eyes…something about the way she looked at him… He had the naked sensation that she was seeing all the way to his soul.

But she'd given him his marching orders. Whatever her troubles, they no longer concerned him—she'd made that plain enough.

'Oh, I almost forgot…' He pulled out the list of piano bars

and clubs he'd made contact with over the past couple of weeks, set it on the table. 'If you want to give up waitressing you might want to check these out.'

Through his open bedroom window Ben squinted against the morning glare as he watched Carissa pedal her way down the drive, her backpack slung across her shoulders, her perky breasts jiggling under a faded green vest-top.

The jolt to his heart at the sight left him shaken. It should have been lust. Instead, a simple longing he hadn't known existed until he'd come here tugged at him. He clenched his jaw. The sooner he left, the better.

She disappeared from view as she turned onto the road. Anger crept through the sweetness. This was exactly what he'd wanted to avoid. From now on, no emotional ties.

He pulled on jeans, headed to the kitchen. Carissa's absence made it easier to grab that last coffee. While he waited for the kettle to boil, he saw her note saying she'd gone grocery shopping. Not easy without a car, but he shrugged. Not his problem.

The soapy scent from Carissa's shower hung on the air. This woman was a puzzle that warmed him from the inside out. It would be a long time before he got her out of his system. So it made sense to leave before she returned. No last goodbyes. A clean break.

He loaded his car, then checked that the supplies for the renovations he'd started were stored away, took a last look at the new steps, watered the herb garden. He was stalling, and it annoyed him.

When he returned to the house the phone was ringing. He'd decided not to answer it when he remembered Carissa hadn't been looking well again this morning. Perhaps she needed help with the groceries after all. He picked up. 'Good morning.'

'Good morning.' A brisk, businesslike voice answered. 'Is Carissa available?'

'She's not here at present. Can I take a message?' He glanced around for pen and paper.

'This is Della from Dr Sharman's surgery. We've scheduled Carissa's appointment for two o'clock this Thursday. If you could pass the message on, please?'

'Hang on, what's the name again?'

'Dr Elise Sharman.'

He couldn't find any paper, so he scribbled the time and date on the wall. 'I'll be sure to let her know,' he muttered, then disconnected.

Something wasn't right. It had to be a specialist's appointment. He grabbed the phone book and flipped pages till he found it: Dr Elise Sharman. Gynaecology and Obstetrics.

The breath exploded from his lungs. He felt as if a bass guitar had ploughed into his gut. Because his knees were shot he sank to the floor, let his head fall back against the wall. Pregnant. Sweet heaven. She'd kicked him out because she was having a baby.

His baby.

It was one of those moments when everything suddenly seemed intense yet surreal, like the finale at a rock concert when the audience was whipped to a frenzy. The way his heart tripped—different somehow—the cool wall at his back, the threadbare mustard carpet, the odd feeling that he'd stepped into someone else's life.

And finally, a sense of betrayal. She'd not told him. Had she ever intended to? Did she think he valued his freedom above responsibility?

The man with no roots, no place to call home, accountable to no one but himself. Wasn't that what he did best? Hadn't he proved that over and over? To his mum and himself and others? To Carissa?

Pushing up, he dragged a hand over the back of his neck and scowled at the bare room. Not a bar in sight when you needed one. The kitchen didn't offer much more, but he found a Diet Pepsi at the back of the fridge behind the milk, popped the top, then sat at the table to wait.

* * *

Carissa took the long way home. She dreaded the final goodbye and was momentarily tempted to take the coward's way out and cycle to Mel's for the rest of the day until she was sure the coast was clear. But she wasn't going to back away from this, no matter how she felt. And she didn't feel good, in more ways than one.

The sun had lost summer's sting but the heat still had enough punch to suck away her already depleted energy. Her pack of supplies weighed hot and heavy on her back and the smell of someone's oily cooking wafted across the road.

A sudden nausea churned in her stomach and climbed up her throat. Her lips felt like chalk as she pressed them together and fought it down. She needed to get home before she disgraced herself on the side of the road.

Her heart did a fast staccato when she saw the Porsche. A crisp breeze with the faint tang of salt teased her hair and cooled the sweat as she parked her bike at the side of the house and let herself inside.

She came to an abrupt and startled halt at the kitchen door. She'd expected Ben to be in his room, not sitting at her kitchen table. With bloodshot eyes, tousled hair and a Pepsi can in his hand. His face could have been carved from granite. A blind woman stood as much chance of reading his expression.

She wanted nothing more than to crawl onto her bed and close her eyes, but sleep wasn't an option until he'd gone. She lowered her pack to the floor. 'Hi.'

Ben didn't move, but his eyes shifted from her face and travelled down her body, coming to rest on her belly. Her traitorous stomach muscles clenched and she had to fight to keep her hands loose at her sides.

He *couldn't* know. But her pulse drummed dangerously, the kitchen spun and she slid loosely into the chair opposite him before she fell.

'You weren't going to tell me, were you?' Ben drained the can, set it on the table with a firm 'clunk.' Cool green eyes glinted as he leaned back.

She dragged air into her lungs, opened her mouth to speak, closed it again. Panic was beating its way out of her chest. He knew. Somehow he knew.

'You were just going to let me walk. In fact you made it your business to see that I did.'

She tried to clear her throat but it was as dry as the Nullabor.

'*Miz* Independence.' The way he said it made it sound like one of the seven deadly sins. In a carefully controlled movement, he closed a fist around the empty can, squeezed till it crumpled like paper. 'Do you figure this is only about you?'

'I—'

He cut her off with a slash of his hand. 'It's about us. Us and *our baby.*'

Because her hands were shaking, she clasped them together beneath the table and wished herself a thousand miles away, preferably on a bed. 'I intended to tell you. Later. I needed time to think, to get used to the idea first. To decide what to do.'

'And what did *you* decide?'

'I will have the baby, if that's what you're asking. Beyond that…I…' Any further thoughts lay crushed beneath the force of that gaze of stone. But his eyes—she had to force herself to meet them—swirled with a jumble of emotions.

They watched one another for seconds that stretched into eternity. She heard the steady drip-drip of the leaky tap, the hum of the refrigerator, the rapid thump of her heart.

'I've had a couple of hours to think too,' he said at last. 'I'll tell you what we're going to do. We're getting married.'

'Married?' The word, the very idea sent a spasm of nerves twisting up her spine. 'I don't think so.' She pushed up from the table and moved to the sink to splash water on her cheeks before she faced him.

If it was possible, his face had hardened further, and there was a steely determination in his eyes tempered with something like understanding. A sense of connection rocked her. She wanted to drop onto those hard thighs, bury her face against that chest and let herself lean. Instead she said, 'I don't need you making decisions for me. I can get along just fine on my own.'

'You're not on your own anymore.'

He was right; she knew already. She had a child to consider. For once she had to put independence and pride aside for the sake of the baby. How could she provide for another when she could barely get by herself?

'We'll get married as soon as we can get the paperwork done,' he said.

'I'm not ready for marriage.'

His brow lifted. 'Hadn't you been planning just that when we met?' His eyes narrowed. 'Do you still have feelings for the guy?'

'No.' How could she when she suddenly knew with absolute certainty she was in love with the man in front of her? *In love.* She'd thought she knew that emotion, but it had never felt like this, an ache that filled her body to overflowing.

And it broke her heart.

'This…it's so…calculated,' she said, her voice hoarse. 'Like a business transaction.'

'If it doesn't work out we can always get a divorce.'

That he could talk so casually of marriage and divorce in the same breath made her want to cry. 'That's not the kind of life I want, for me or my baby.'

'*Our* baby.' His expression softened with those words, but he still had that steel in his eyes. 'I don't want you to do this alone, Carissa. You don't have the funds or the support.'

He was right, but she didn't want to think about it this minute, *couldn't* think about it. 'I can't talk to you now. Mel's coming over after she gets off duty, then I've got to go to work. I'd appreciate it if you could give Mel and me some time alone so I can explain all this.'

'No waiting tables until after the baby's born. No more waiting tables, period. My wife—'

'Now listen up, Mr Fame and Fortune, this is my life we're talking about, and I didn't agree to enter a life of submission. And if you think I'll give up work on your say-so, think again. If the doctor says its okay, I'm working.'

He watched her a moment, nodded slowly. 'Fair enough. For now. From your answer I take it that you agreed to my proposal.'

'Of marriage? Is that what it was? As marriage proposals go, I'd say there's lots of room for improvement.'

Stupidly, impossibly hurt by his offhand manner and the way he was laying down conditions, she made for the door and sanctuary of her room. But as she brushed past him his hand shot out, curled around her arm.

'Carissa, wait.' The heat of his palm burned into her skin. His eyes were clear and green and she was stunned to see the depth of honesty and openness. 'We don't have a lot between us now, but what we do have is good. I've never asked a woman to marry me, and I don't expect to do it again.'

The dull, sweet ache sharpened as the implication penetrated. 'What would you expect from our marriage?'

'You'll give me an anchor, something to hold on to. I understand you well enough to know you'll meet me halfway and you'll be faithful. In return I'll give you wealth and security— and think about it—even if you don't want my money, you'll be able to keep this house, and give the child what it deserves. And no one and nothing will come before the two of you. That I can promise you.'

What about love? she wanted to ask. But all those things he'd offered counted for a heck of a lot. She nodded slowly, meeting his eyes. 'Okay. But I want something in writing.'

Something to protect herself when things fell apart. *Stop right there.* Where was her optimism when she needed it most? Why should she fail any more than anybody else who took vows they intended to keep? He was the realist, and he was prepared to give it a go.

But unlike him, she was laying her heart at his feet, leaving herself wide open to having it broken. If only he knew. Well, he wasn't going to find out that little piece of information.

He let her go. 'Fine. We'll draft something together. By the way, we have an appointment with Dr Sharman on Thursday at 2:00 p.m. I assume you know where that is?'

So that was it. The damn phone. *Everything happens for a reason.* 'We? No, I don't—'

'Don't even try leaving me out of it. I'm coming and that's a fact.'

His expression was not at all loverlike as they eyed each other in the silence that followed. No shared happiness over the news that they were going to be parents. No celebratory dinner for two planned or excited phone calls to relatives.

She hugged her arms. 'Is this really what you want?'

'I could ask you the same question. I guess we'll find out together. I'll leave you to work out the details you want for the ceremony. I'm not bothered how we do it.'

He wasn't bothered? He'd told her he wasn't a for ever guy. Did he intend to stay on here in one place, to stay faithful, as he obviously thought she would? She was afraid to ask. She was better off not knowing.

She was taking the biggest risk of her life. And so, she thought, was he. She wondered who stood to lose the most from this deal.

CHAPTER EIGHT

'MEL.' Carissa hugged her stepsister at the door, clung for a moment, breathing in the strawberry scent of her hair before stepping back to let her in. 'Thanks for coming over at short notice.'

'You sounded different on the phone,' Mel said, studying Carissa's face. 'Something's happened. Let me guess.' A teasing smile lit her eyes. 'Mr Music's asked you to marry him and he's going to whisk you away to a life of luxury.'

Carissa turned away, gave herself a few seconds before facing her again. 'It wasn't so much a question as a statement of intent.'

'What was?' Melanie settled on the sofa and clasped her fingers around one raised knee.

Because her legs were shaky, Carissa opted for the piano stool. 'Ben's...' she lifted a shoulder '...proposal.'

Mel shifted from casual to full alert and leaned forward. 'Proposal,' she said slowly. 'As in marriage?' If it hadn't been so serious it would have been comical. 'You and Ben? Oh, Carrie, I'm sorry. I stole your thunder. I was joking. I wanted to get a rise out of you.'

'Believe me, it's no joke.'

'I had no idea.' With a whoop, she jumped up, lunged across the room and hugged her.

Carissa remained sitting and struggled against the urge to cry.

She wished she could have been happy. Instead she was afraid and unsure and still numb with shock.

'So why the long face?' Mel pulled back and her grey eyes turned serious. 'You look like he asked you to cut off your piano-playing fingers. You accepted?'

'I told you it wasn't a question.'

'No one can force you, Carrie. First off, do you love him?'

Admitting what her heart had known for some time was a big, new and scary step. She swiped her eyes and nodded.

'So what's the problem? And why the tears, for heaven's sake? Hey, if he didn't ask the way you wanted, maybe it's because he doesn't know how.'

'Or maybe it's because he doesn't want to marry me at all.'

'Then why would he ask, silly? I've seen the way he looks at you. And I don't think a man like Ben would do anything he doesn't want to.'

If only Carissa could be sure that was true. 'I'm pregnant.' Suddenly she couldn't sit still. She paced to the window. A flock of galahs had descended on the gum tree, their raucous cries shattering the stunned stillness.

'You were supposed to use the condoms,' Mel said behind her. 'Take it from me, they're not fail-safe.'

'Just a moment...' Mel's hands came to rest on Carissa's shoulders and she turned her around until they stood eye to narrowed eye. 'You've only known him, what, since mid-February? Just how pregnant are you?'

'Seven weeks. Dr Beaton gave me the good news yesterday. A one-night stand, Mel. Remember, you thought it was a good idea at the time.'

'Sure, with protection. I didn't think you'd actually go through with it on a whim. Not you, not steady-as-she-goes, think-every-thing-over-twice, predictable Carissa.'

'Not exactly a whim. I thought it over for at least an hour.'

Mel blew out an incredulous breath. 'An hour.'

'I saw and used an opportunity. And it felt right. But I trapped him, Mel. He doesn't want this baby.'

'Did he tell you that?'

'No.'

In fact she'd given him the perfect opportunity to simply disappear. He could have taken off after that phone call he'd intercepted and never looked back. But he hadn't. Didn't that tell her something about the man?

'There you are, then,' Mel said, and squeezed Carissa's shoulders.

'He comes with baggage. He's mourning his friend, blames himself. He won't discuss his family. He's involved in some sort of business but doesn't talk about it. He's obviously wealthy—what if he's involved in something illegal?'

'Do you really think that?'

Carissa sighed, knowing deep down Ben was a man of integrity. 'He's still a mystery man.'

'Look, sis, it may not be the love affair of the millennium, but if he's willing to take responsibility and make a go of it, even if only for the baby's sake, I'd say you're one lucky girl.' Mel turned to the kitchen. 'Where is this knight of yours and soon-to-be brother-in-law?'

'I wanted to talk to you alone.'

Carissa remained by the window. Ben's Porsche was still in the garage. Presumably he'd walked to the beach. She wondered how he was feeling, what he was thinking. Was he as devastated as she? He hadn't looked it; he'd looked determined and in control.

'When are you going to do it?'

'A week.' She set her jaw. 'No fuss, just you and Adam, and if Ben wants anyone special... There's his mum, of course...' Her heart squeezed in sympathy when she remembered his loss. 'Oh, Mel...his friend.'

'Then small and simple's the way to go.'

'We'll have it here. In this room.'

'Here?' Mel's frown said it all, but she raised a smile when she saw Carissa was serious. 'That could work...with some time and money. A lot of money. Maybe Ben could—'

'No. Definitely not. No way. It's take me as I am, cracks-in-the-wall and all. Ben's prepared to be a father for my baby—'

'He *is* the father, Carrie.'

The sharp, sweet pain of acknowledgement stabbed at Carissa's heart. 'I can't ask for more than that.'

'Honey, it's your *wedding*. And it's his wedding, too.'

'It's not a wedding. It's an exchange of words.'

Mel raised her palms. 'Whatever you say.'

Ben hadn't shown one iota of interest in the details, so it was as Mel said—whatever Carissa wanted. She thought of the wedding magazines she pored over, the gown she'd designed, the little church her grandmother had been married in, then put them out of her mind.

'Maybe he'll turn up in those hip-hugging, ball-breaking leather pants the band wears,' Mel said, eyes twinkling.

'Oh, God.' That poster. 'I don't know him at all—what am I getting myself into?'

'Calm down, I'm teasing. Underneath he's just a regular guy—a rich and *gorgeous* regular guy.'

The mention of *underneath* had Carissa's mind flashing back to that night. To the huge, hard masculine part of him that had gotten her into this predicament. Its dark and sensual beauty as he slid it inside her, his hot skin rubbing her nipples... She shivered. *Underneath,* he was no ordinary guy.

But he was marrying her for the baby's sake. Nothing more. And was that enough? Would it ever be enough?

As a distraction, she moved to the piano and belted out the first stirring bars of 'Phantom of the Opera.' For all their sakes, she hoped she wasn't making the biggest mistake of her life.

Ben returned from his jog on the beach to find Carissa in a frenzy of domestic activity. She was slicing fruit salad, something spicy simmered on the stove. She had an hour before she had to go to work.

'I hope you're eating some of that before you go.'

She squeezed passion-fruit pulp and lemon juice into the bowl. 'No, I'll grab a snack later.'

'I told you not to cook for me.' He frowned, suddenly aware of her paler complexion, the smudges beneath her eyes. 'Snacks aren't enough in your condition.' *Leave it be,* he warned himself. Grabbing a chair, he turned it around and straddled it. 'You talked to Melanie?'

'Yes.'

'And?'

Carissa squeezed detergent into the sink, turned on the taps full blast and began washing dishes. 'She's looking forward to getting to know her new brother-in-law.'

He felt a weight lift. At least Melanie was on his side, but Carissa had her back to him and he had no idea how to read her. 'What have you decided about the ceremony?'

'I thought we could have it in the living room. I've already asked Mel and Adam. I know a marriage celebrant if she's available at such short notice.' The sound of pots clunking in water filled the brief silence. 'Who do you want to ask?'

'No one.' Jess wouldn't want the reminder.

'What about your mum?'

He hesitated. 'There's something I haven't told you about Mum. She's in a home. Hasn't spoken in ten years.'

Carissa turned, her eyes full of sympathy. 'Oh. I'm sorry.'

The old ache that struck whenever he thought of his mother squeezed his heart. Instinctively he rubbed the heel of his hand over his chest. 'So am I.' She'd have been ecstatic watching him marry a class act like Carissa.

'Carissa, if we're having it here, I'd like to…' Melanie would be easier to approach and he could do a bit of manoeuvring. 'Do something for me. Wear blue, something long and slim.'

She muttered something as she pulled the plug. Water drained with an ominous glugging sound.

'I'm paying for the dress, so no talk about not being able to afford it. If we're getting married, we share, and that means sharing expenses, as crass as the mention of money might sound to you. And I'm calling a plumber.'

He saw her shoulders droop and something uneasy worked through him. Was she thinking of another wedding she'd planned? Did she have a chaste white gown stashed away with her unfulfilled dreams? 'Wear whatever you want,' he said more gruffly than he should have.

'I haven't given my wardrobe a thought. I've more important things on my mind. But thank you.' She wiped her hands on a cloth. 'You do own a suit, I assume? I know it's only a small gathering, but…'

'I won't let you down, Carissa.' He realised then how much he wanted to believe it.

He'd give it his best shot; for his child, for Carissa, and for the memory of the boy trying to win a father's love that had never existed in the first place.

After he'd dropped Carissa at work, he rang Melanie, got her address and headed over.

'Hi, Ben. Come on in. I'm glad you called. I'm busy plotting and need your opinion. By the way, welcome to the family, such as it is.' Melanie pecked his cheek, then showed him into the living room where she'd spread paint chips and cloth swatches over every available surface.

'Redecorating?'

'Yes, but not here, this is for Carissa.'

He nodded, pleased he'd trusted his instincts with Melanie. 'Just what I want to discuss. I'd like to do something with the living room before the wedding but I don't want Carissa getting stressed out over it.'

'Of course not.'

He stuck his hands in his pockets. 'We'll have to get her out of the house for a few days.'

'I'll insist she stay here. A girl's last days of freedom should be with family. She'll go for it—I'll make sure. Trust me. I'll ask Adam to help you.'

'I want to hire a painter, if you could choose the furnishings—you know her taste. Then there's the catering and…'

Melanie picked up a pad and pen and smiled. 'Okay, sit down and let's make a list.'

Clutching a bouquet of white roses, Carissa stepped from the limo Ben had organised to collect her, Mel and Adam. 'I don't know if I can go through with this.' She smoothed a clammy hand down the ice-blue silk sheath and wished she felt as cool, calm and collected as Mel looked in her fuschia-trimmed emerald dress.

'You'll be fine when you see Ben,' Mel assured her. 'You'll both be fine. Adam told me Ben's as uptight as you are.'

Ben. She was marrying Ben. Her stomach heaved, and for a moment the house shimmered before her eyes. She clutched her belly. *Don't do this to me, little one. Your father wouldn't understand.*

A cool breeze kissed her cheeks and the nausea passed. The day was a perfect blue. Someone whistled and honked their horn as a car whizzed by.

Nerves were doing a fast rumba in her belly and she fingered one of the rosebuds Mel had twisted into her upswept hair. 'I feel ridiculous, all dressed up going into my own living room.'

'Pretend it's a chapel.' Mel laid a hand on Carissa's elbow. 'Give Adam a minute to open the door.'

She grasped Mel's arm. 'Adam's got a video camera.'

'You want a memento of the day, don't you?'

The first strains of a harp rippled through the air, something *olde worlde* and infinitely beautiful. Carissa could smell gardenias and fresh paint. 'There's one of those wedding horseshoe things over the door.' Her pulse shot up and she caught Mel's eyes twinkling. 'I knew I shouldn't have left Ben here alone. What's he done?'

'Planned you a wedding day you'll always remember.'

Tears of emotion threatened to engulf her. 'You were in on this, weren't you?'

But Mel brushed that off. 'It's time. And for God's sake—and Ben's—smile.'

Carissa had to make a conscious effort to relax her lips, and had just gotten that under control when she halted at the door and looked into what had once been her living room. She turned to Mel, but the traitor only smiled and moved past her.

The walls were a warm cream shot with buttercup, the carpet had been ripped up and the floorboards gleamed like warm honey. An oriental rug in rich gold lay in the centre of the room. A harpist played beside the piano. Carissa counted four urns of flowers. White and gold helium balloons with gold strings hovered on the ceiling.

Through a mist, her eyes locked with Ben's. He stood beside the piano in a white shirt, formal grey suit and tie, with a white rose in his lapel, fulfilling all the fantasies she'd ever had about her wedding day. She swallowed the lump in her throat and had to take two deep breaths before she trusted herself to move. She only hoped she wouldn't throw up on the new rug.

His gaze didn't leave her. Oddly, it gave her strength as she crossed the room. She felt as if she were walking in a dream. Finally she stood in front of him. He smelled of peppermints and some spicy new cologne.

'Hi there, Blue Lady,' he whispered. 'Ready?'

She lifted her chin, drowning in the unexpected depth of softness in his eyes. 'I'm ready if you are.'

His mouth, which had remained solemn, curved. 'Then let's get married.'

She put her trembling hand into his outstretched one and the tension melted away in the warmth of his touch.

They moved together, past the harpist, past Mel and Adam, to the celebrant.

'Good morning.' She smiled at them, then began to read from the notes Carissa and Ben had prepared.

'We are here today to witness and share in a marriage ceremony. Marriage is the establishment of a home where through tolerance, patience, courage and understanding two people can develop a strong and lasting relationship with each other and any children they may have. Carissa's and Ben's choice is responsible, free and independent.'

Carissa tried to concentrate on the words, but all she was aware of was the rock-solid comfort of the hand holding hers, the scent of the flowers mingling with Ben's cologne, the quiet cascade of harp strings.

'Marriage according to law in Australia is the union of a man and a woman to the exclusion of all others, voluntarily entered into for life...'

The words pulled her back to the present. This was for real. For life. *If it doesn't work out we can get a divorce.*

Then they were repeating the vows that would bind them. The celebrant asked for the rings. Ben slipped not only the simple gold band she'd chosen, but a second, studded with diamonds and deep sapphires, onto her finger. 'Carissa Mary, I give you these rings as a symbol of the vows we've made this day.'

Then it was her turn. As she slid the Celtic-designed band on his finger and looked into those deep green eyes she wondered fleetingly how long he'd wear it, then the celebrant was pronouncing them husband and wife.

Ben held her face between his hands as if he held the most fragile china. 'Hello, Mrs Jamieson.'

'Mr Jamieson.' *I love you.* How long before she could find the courage to say the words aloud?

How long before she heard them back?

The moment hung like a jewel on a chain of gold. She

absorbed the scent of flowers and Ben, the cascade of watery music, his fingertips against her skin.

His lips touched hers, firm but gentle. She heard Mel's sigh, Adam clearing his throat, before Ben stepped back, his smile reflected in his gaze. Bronze highlights glinted in his newly trimmed deep brown hair.

Melanie was the first to break the moment. She moved in to kiss Carissa, then Ben. 'Congratulations.'

'The man's a lucky guy,' Adam said, dropping a light kiss on Carissa's cheek.

The celebrant stayed for the first glass of bubbly. Carissa toasted with soda water. The harpist entertained them with light classical while they ate a luncheon of prawn and avocado cocktails and chicken and salad, courtesy of the Three Steps. Mel had baked a white chocolate cake.

Carissa couldn't believe where the time had gone when the harpist packed and left and Mel, too, announced she and Adam were leaving.

'But it's only two o'clock.' A fist of nerves gripped her. It would be just the two of them, alone. Which was ridiculous when apart from the past few days they'd shared the same house for weeks.

Mel's eyes danced. 'You'll find what Ben has planned much more exciting,' she promised, and gave her a quick hug. Carissa wanted to hold on, but Mel tugged out of her grasp and almost danced to the door. 'And don't worry about the cleaning-up. I'll be over later.'

'Later?'

'Have a wonderful time. Let's go, Adam.'

Adam and Ben exchanged grins as they shook hands.

'She's bossy, that one,' Carissa told Adam as he leaned in for a kiss.

'I know. Take care.'

'Bossy? Who, me?' Melanie gave him a playful shove and they were out the door in ten seconds flat.

Carissa watched them get into the taxi and drive away. 'That was a little like being hit by a whirlwind,' she murmured.

'That's because we have a plane to catch.'

'A plane?' she said on a rising note of panic. 'I don't even own a suitcase. I can't possibly...'

'Before you say anything, just listen.' Ben's hands rested lightly on her shoulders as he turned her. 'We need some time away in a neutral environment. I've spoken to your boss. Rosie and the crew will work your shifts for a few days. Melanie'll be keeping an eye on the place and she's packed you a bag. The taxi'll be here in half an hour, so you've got time to slip into something more comfortable for travelling.'

'Where are we going?'

'You'll see when we get there.'

'I only hope I won't spoil it for you. Morning sickness. Don't believe the label, it hits at all hours.'

'Then this'll be good for you. You can sleep all day if you want. No one'll disturb you.'

Did he include himself in that promise? She wondered for the hundredth time whether he intended consummating their marriage. He hadn't attempted to touch her since he'd learned of her pregnancy, as if she were a changed person somehow. And sex with commitment—that was something else again.

Before she could ponder that he stepped back. 'But first, I want a good look at you in that gown.' His gaze warmed as surely as if he'd stroked a hand over her body. She felt...desired, cherished, though she knew it was only the power of the day, the euphoria she felt for the moment.

He'd married her, but he didn't love her.

But he'd made it so, so special. 'Thank you. For everything. I had no idea, even when Mel insisted I stay over.'

'I'm glad you enjoyed it.'

It was easy to take that step forward, to rest her hands against his chest. He'd removed his suit jacket and the scent and heat of his skin warmed her palms through the crisp cotton shirt. Her rings glittered in the light.

He bent and met her lips, brushed them, once, twice, before moving lightly to nip at her throat. 'I have to tell you, I have this thing for women with slender exposed necks.' Her head fell back as his hands slid into her hair and his lips moved like slow honey over her neck. 'Drives me crazy.'

Oh, my... 'Did you mention a taxi?' she managed to murmur.

'Yeah. And now I've messed your hair.' He tried to finger-comb it back without much success. 'And after you had it salon-done.'

'Hey, I did it myself. Mel helped me.'

'I left you money. Wasn't it enough?'

'I didn't use it. I'm not used to spending on a whim.'

He frowned. 'Well, get used to it. You married rich, Mrs Jamieson.'

She shook her hair and tugged at pins, annoyed that he'd brought the subject up. 'I didn't marry you for money.'

His eyes darkened. 'No. I guess you didn't.' He stepped back and stuck his hands in his pockets. 'Better go get ready.'

She nodded, backing away, aware she'd hurt him somehow and unsure how to fix it.

She'd never given a honeymoon a thought, but now, as she slipped out of the silk gown and into light trousers and sweater, she almost felt a sense of relief. No awkward wondering whether he'd sleep in his room or come to her bed. What would happen, would happen. Or not.

After a quick briefing with Joe, the pilot, Ben settled down beside Carissa for the flight to Mackay. From there they'd catch a helicopter to the island.

As the tiny sleek jet lifted into the air he watched her nerves turn to awe. Late-afternoon sun slanted through a gap in the thickening cloud and glinted off the wing, and as they banked it caught her hair, now in a braid over one shoulder, setting it ablaze in a rope of gold.

Her knuckles whitened on the arm rest as the plane hit minor turbulence rising through the clouds. 'Nothing to see for a while,' he reassured her. 'Relax and try to get some rest.'

Then it was all smooth sailing and clouds. Her eyes closed and soon her head lolled back. He popped the top on a beer and settled back to enjoy the brief hiatus.

She was his wife, soon to be the mother of his child, yet they were strangers. Married strangers. Their lives travelled different paths. Even for starry-eyed couples in love, it was a gamble.

He looked at his sleeping wife and something soft yet fierce tugged at him. Everything had already changed. For once in his life he'd hit the jackpot with Carissa and a wise gambler knew when the stakes were too high to risk.

CHAPTER NINE

THE tropical evening was alive with insect noise when they arrived at the Black Opal Resort, Emerald Island, on the Great Barrier Reef. Ben led Carissa along a path lined with palms and kerosene torches. Island music drifted on the air.

She gazed up at the glittering entrance. 'Wow.'

Her wide-eyed wonder made him smile. He turned his smile to the woman in the floral uniform waiting to welcome them in the lobby, then bent forward to kiss her cheek. 'Hi, Tahlia, good to see you again.'

'Ben, congratulations! I was so excited when I heard the news.'

Carissa's eyes were glazed over with fatigue as Ben smoothed a reassuring hand down her back. 'Tahlia, I'd like you to meet Carissa. My wife.'

'Mrs Jamieson.' Tahlia turned that familiar smile on Carissa. 'Congratulations, and welcome. If I can be of service for anything at all, let me know.'

'Thank you. I'm sure everything'll be wonderful.'

'You're in the Orchid Garden villa, as requested,' she informed Ben. 'Simon'll bring your bags.'

'Thanks, Tahlia. We'll make our own way.'

'So you're a regular guest here,' Carissa said as they strolled from the four-storey building towards the villas nestled among palms and lush gardens. 'I can see why. It's gorgeous.'

She slowed near a row of scarlet hibiscus, but he tugged her along the path. 'Come on, you're so tired you can barely walk straight. We'll explore tomorrow.'

'I think I'm sleepwalking and I'm having this wonderful dream.'

She was swaying as he decoded the door then led her inside to a wicker couch. 'Here, sit a moment.'

The ubiquitous bowl of tropical fruits and bottle of sparkling white and two glasses sat on a glass table. 'Mangoes, yum.' She picked one up and sniffed. 'Sorry, no wine for me.'

'I'll order something. Soda water okay?'

At her nod he rang Room Service, then moved through the suite, opening windows and drapes. The sounds and scents of the tropics drifted in on the heavy air. A fountain trickled by their private patio lit by a green lantern. Beyond, the languorous sounds of a sheltered sea calmed the soul. He turned on an overhead fan to set a lazy draught.

'I prefer the outdoors, but if you'd rather the air-con, I can...' He trailed off when he realised she wasn't listening. Something stirred in him as he watched her sleep, one hand under her cheek on the arm of the couch. Something big, something awesome, something downright scary.

He'd never felt it before, this cocktail of sexual desire and heartbreaking tenderness, and it brought a God-awful lump to his throat. Left him shaken, left his brain incapable of rational thought.

Their bags arrived with the water, sparing him the task of dwelling on his emotions. When the bellboy had gone, he crouched down in front of Carissa. Her slow breathing warmed his face. She was wearing some exotic perfume he'd never smelled on her before today, something mysterious and evocative. It reminded him of blooms that flowered only by the light of the moon.

He slipped his arms beneath her and she slid bonelessly against him. Switching the lights off, he moved through the quiet rooms and laid her on the bed. Moonlight poured through the window, gilding her features. He slipped off her shoes and wondered about removing her outer garments or whether she'd wake and think he was making a move on her.

So he left her and took a quick shower. A cold, quick shower. For tonight at least, to spare her the sight of his over-eager masculinity, he pulled on a pair of boxers rather then his usual habit of sleeping naked.

It wouldn't have made a difference; she was still asleep when he returned. Easing onto the bed beside her, he took a deep breath and wondered how many nights he'd lie like this in the darkness—wanting her, waiting for her to want him.

Her gut-wrenching groan had him fumbling for the lamp.

She pushed up, a hand over her mouth. Her face was chalk-white. 'Bathroom,' she whimpered, and rolled off the bed.

'Here.' He shot up, ready to help, but, ignoring him, she stumbled across the room, slammed the door in his face.

He hurried to grab a soda and glass, then knocked at the door. 'You okay?'

'What do you think?' Anger and impatience in that raw-throated voice.

'I've got some—'

'Go away. Go far, far away.'

He backed up. 'Okay.'

Feeling helpless and—dammit—responsible, he put the drink on the bedside table and moved to the patio and let the breeze touch his body. Probably the only touching he was likely to get any time soon.

How long did she have to put up with this sickness? He had no idea. He heard the toilet flush, the sound of running water, then the door opened.

He stood still, hesitant to approach her. 'You look like death on a warming dish.'

'Thank you. A bride loves to hear compliments like that on her wedding night. I feel much better now.' She waved a hand towards the door. 'Is that a private bathroom or do we have to share with the entire island? That spa's a lake, and the jungle of potted palms...' Colour was seeping back into her cheeks. She picked up her glass. 'Thanks.'

She eyed him with a trace of humour. 'One of us is over-dressed here.' She unzipped her bag, rummaged through it and pulled out something white and lacy, then disappeared into the bathroom again.

He turned out the light, slid between the sheets and waited. His blood pounded through his groin with a need that bordered on pain.

That need doubled when she opened the door and made her way towards the bed. In the dimness he could see her body outlined against the shimmering silk. Its pale sheen high-lighted the shadows beneath her breasts, the darker nipples. He swallowed over a dry throat, his eyes moving lower to the triangle of hair.

All too well he could imagine lifting that barely there hem and pushing it up and up over her thighs... Sliding a finger into that warm moisture, dropping to his knees and tasting it on his tongue... A groan rumbled in his chest. He was rock-hard and ready to roll.

He closed his eyes. Then he mentally recited the national anthem. Backwards. Told himself she needed rest. He didn't move when the bed dipped a little as she slowly slid in beside him.

'Ben?' Barely a whisper.

She was close enough for the heat of her luscious body to torture him, but not so close that they touched. In the dark he almost smiled at the irony. She was trying not to wake *him*.

He lay for a long time listening to the night sounds and his own body's galloping thump, willing his erection to subside. Not a chance.

Something moved in the garden outside, a lizard, maybe. He heard the muted sound of music from the open-air cabaret and the slap of water on sand beyond their villa, Carissa's slow breathing.

Finally, as he drifted on the edge of sleep, he thought he heard a voice whisper, 'Thank you, Ben.'

His lips curved in the grey tropical night. *My pleasure, Carissa Mary.*

Carissa rolled over and out of bed and stumbled straight to the bathroom. What a way to spend a honeymoon. She moistened a cloth and wiped her mouth. Still, you weren't supposed to *be* pregnant on your honeymoon. She stood up and stretched, revelling in the sun filtering through the skylight and onto the indoor garden. Amazing how you could feel so lousy one moment, so good the next.

Ben was asleep, sprawled on one side when she returned. His left hand dangled over the bed, wedding ring still attached. The sheet covered him just where it began to get interesting, below the arrow of dark hair beneath his navel.

His broad bare chest rose and fell with each breath. So tempting to reach out and run her fingers through the spattering of dark hair. To lave her tongue over the flat, pebbly nipple, take it between her teeth and tug.

She couldn't drag her gaze away. The stress lines that often furrowed his face had smoothed out. He looked younger. And innocent. She felt an unfamiliar and overwhelming tenderness, a warm tide that left her weak and wanting.

Then he rolled onto his back with a stertorous sigh and the sheet slipped low. Very low.

Oh…mmm. He was stretched out on the bed like a feast and her mouth watered. Even semi-aroused he was big. The blood raced through her body, its sultry heat causing drops of perspiration to form on her brow, between her breasts. As if by the power of lustful thoughts his erection grew, shooting sparks along her arteries.

This man was her husband. As his wife, all that masculinity belonged to her and her alone. Possessiveness wasn't something she was familiar with either, but it was there, lodged firmly inside her. Something she'd have to overcome sooner or later.

He'd leave eventually. Why would he want an inexperienced woman like herself when he probably had a lover in every Australian state? A classical pianist when he wrote music for a rock band? Better to get used to the idea of loss.

His eyes snapped open, rather suddenly, for someone who'd supposedly been asleep. 'Good morning.' He stretched, unashamedly naked, stomach muscles rippling, the thick jut of his sex angling her way as he drew up a knee and put his hands behind his head.

'Good morning.' She walked to the patio to drink in a less unsettling picture. Through the lush green outside, sunlight danced on white sand and turquoise sea. The atmosphere breathed sounds and fragrances. Life, vitality. 'Such a beautiful view.'

'Not bad from here either.'

Licks of heat slid over her skin. In the full light of day and her sheer nightgown she was barely decent. 'I'll order up breakfast. What would you like?' As she spoke she moved to her bag and pulled out the slinky white robe Mel had packed to cover herself.

'Anything. Everything. Leave it off. I like looking at you. You remind me of a fairy-tale princess with the morning light on your shoulders and your hair tumbled.'

But he wasn't looking at her shoulders or her hair. A nervous laugh threatened. Instead she said, 'You've a way with words. You're a musician. Put them to music.' She put the robe down and refolded her travelling clothes to busy her hands.

'My songwriting days are over.' He punched his pillow, frowned up at the ceiling.

It distressed her to hear his sadness. 'You'll write new songs, better ones.'

'I'm dried up.'

She heard the resignation in his voice and wanted, suddenly, to shake him out of that hole he'd dug himself into. 'So get out the hose. You're good at that.'

'I'm hungry,' he said, dismissing her suggestion with a hand on his stomach. 'Why don't you order up that breakfast you suggested?'

She glared at him. 'You've not heard the last of this.' But she picked up the phone. 'Yes, good morning. This is the Orchard Garden villa.'

Twenty minutes later they were tucking into fresh fruit, croissants and coffee. She felt like a film star surrounded by luxury.

'What do you want to do today?' Ben slid a brochure across the table. 'We can take a glass-bottom boat and view the coral, scuba dive or take a walk through the rainforest.'

No suggestion of spending it in bed. Carissa rolled her shoulders, feeling the sunlight sparking off greenery by their patio while she filled her lungs with sea air and told herself she was *not* disappointed. 'I'll let the expert decide.'

'Okay. I suggest we take one of their famous gourmet hampers over to one of the little islands by dinghy. We can unwind with a massage after and enjoy our own private spa before dinner.'

'You've already done those things here, haven't you?' With some other woman, some other lover. An ache settled near her heart, but she took a slice of melon, bit into its sweetness.

'Not with my wife.' He set his knife down and met her eyes. 'The night you walked into my life I was a different man.'

She shook her head. 'Not true, Ben. You never intended to see me again. I certainly didn't intend seeing *you* again.'

'Maybe it started out that way. Do you remember what you wore that night?'

'My one and only. My blue gown.'

'What else?'

'Nothing. Oh…' She felt the tell-tale blush creep into her cheeks.

'A skimpy blue triangle that had me fantasising over you for the next few weeks. Something I'm still doing.' His voice was bland, hiding whatever feelings he had regarding their yet-to-be-consummated marriage, but his eyes turned molten, holding hers for several long heartbeats.

'Ben…'

'It wasn't just about sex.' He opened a croissant and spread it with jam. 'You got to me.'

His words sent a thrill through her, but she knew it cost him to admit it. 'Me too,' she said softly. 'The night before we got together, out the front of the hotel you were so in control, all anger and impatience. I imagined how…satisfying it would be to turn all that masculine energy to my advantage.'

He picked up his coffee-cup and kicked back in his chair, assessing her with deceptively lazy interest. 'Did your thoughts run to how you might achieve your goal, by any chance?'

'I may have been a virgin, but I have a rich imagination.'

That awful word again, the one that reminded her of her inexperience in the bedroom, that told her she wasn't Ben's ideal woman. Her upbeat mood deflated.

'Ben, if you ever…' Because she didn't want to look at him, she poured a second coffee that she didn't want. 'Our marriage is a partnership, a coming together to raise a child, so if you do ever want to… I'll understand, but I'd rather not know. But I would ask you to keep it discreet. I don't want to be an object of ridicule or pity.'

A gentle breeze with the scent of salt and green blew off the sea, cooling her suddenly heated face.

'Carissa.' He leaned forward, captured her hands clenched together on the table. 'Sweetheart…'

'No. Don't say something you'll regret later.' She pulled away and went to rummage in her bag. 'I'm going to take a swim in that pool I saw last night before I get too fat to wear a swimsuit. Meet you there when you're ready.'

She collected what she needed and retreated to the safety of the bathroom to change. With a sigh she lowered herself to the edge of the tub. She'd just given her husband of less than a day permission to go with other women.

He'd not made any attempt to touch her since they'd arrived. Which left her to assume he didn't want her anymore. She lifted a shoulder. So he'd told her he'd fantasised about her. He talked the talk, but did he walk the walk?

She slipped out of her nightie and took a critical inventory of her naked body. Tall, lean, breasts a little undersized, but getting bigger. A wife in name only. Because it hurt and frustrated her, she turned away and wriggled into a sleek black swimsuit, then covered herself with one of the resort's colourful orchid-print beach robes.

Would he ever want her again?

Ben stood on the umbrella-decked patio overlooking the pool where he could see Carissa sliding sunscreen over that long, sleek body. He frowned, his fingers crumpling the hotel's entertainment guide. It should be his hands doing the honours.

He watched as she slipped a strap off her shoulder, innocently provocative, and rubbed in slow, languid movements. She rose, sun gleaming on her skin, as graceful as her maiden name as she sauntered to the edge of the pool and dived in, her streamlined body a blur of black and tan beneath rippling blue water.

'Ben?' The sound of Tahlia's voice didn't distract him from the tempting scene a few metres away.

'What?' he growled.

'What are you doing here by yourself and scowling?'

He shifted, uncomfortable, clenched and unclenched his left hand, noticing the unfamiliar weight of his wedding ring. 'To be honest, I'm not sure.'

'Now there's a change.' She smiled, but concern clouded her eyes. 'Ben, is there anything I can do for you?'

'Can you reserve two masseurs at 5:00 p.m., please, and let's see, an arrangement of orchids delivered to our villa this afternoon. And that tear-drop sapphire necklace in the lobby boutique—I'd like it put in the resort's safe for now.'

She scribbled on her clipboard. 'I'll get right on it. Are you sure everything is okay? I'm asking as a friend.'

'Fine, Tahlia.' He forced a smile. 'I just got married, didn't I? Everything's peachy.'

'Your wife will be glad to hear it.'

'Will she?' he wondered aloud, and couldn't stop his gaze returning to the scene outside. Glistening with water, she'd left the pool and was stretched face-down on a towel.

He felt Tahlia come up beside him, smelled her crisp, fresh scent. 'We've known each other too long, Ben.' Her fingers pressed into his forearm. 'If you want to talk, you know where I am.'

'Thanks.' He covered her hand with one of his, but he didn't take his eyes off the woman by the pool.

Time to find out just how glad she was to see him.

He ordered two mineral waters over ice, then walked slowly to the table beside Carissa, still stretched out, long eyelashes resting on her cheeks. When the water arrived he dipped a finger in one, then crouched down beside her and drew a line of cold moisture down her back.

She shuddered, gasped and rolled over. 'Oh, hi.' Her wary expression softened and he relaxed into a few seconds of sheer pleasure at seeing one of her rare, carefree smiles before the wariness returned.

'Hi.' He bent to drop a kiss on one sun-warmed shoulder, handed her the glass. 'I've come to take my wife on a picnic. Meet me in the lobby in half an hour?'

'Okay.'

He watched her long, lithe limbs as she rose. Every curve was perfection. She smelled of suntan oil and hot female flesh. His groin tightened. His hands itched. He wanted that body against his, under his. Now. It took effort but he remained where he was, having to content himself with the view.

So he wasn't prepared when long fingers dipped into the glass, and before he could duck she'd dropped a lump of ice inside his shirt. 'Hey!'

She drained her glass, picked up her towel and suntan lotion. 'Half an hour,' she tossed over her shoulder as she walked away.

He was gratified to see she still had a sense of humour. Grinning, he went to collect a picnic hamper.

Carissa was waiting in the lobby when she saw Ben and Tahlia approach together. Her fingers tightened on the brim of the sun hat on her lap. She watched him touch Tahlia's arm in an easy way, then head back the way he'd come. Something hot and unwelcome stabbed through her.

The well-groomed brunette smiled and sat down on the sofa beside Carissa, placed her clipboard on her lap. 'Good morning, Mrs Jamieson.'

'Good morning. And, please, the name's Carissa.' She tried to relax, but couldn't stop herself wondering how well Ben and Tahlia knew each other. That hot feeling intensified and she willed the steamy images away.

'Ben forgot the camera. He asked me to keep you company a few moments.'

Carissa sensed a reserve in the voice behind the smile, but she smiled back. 'It must be great working here.'

'It is. So how did you two meet?'

Just the question Carissa had been itching to ask her. 'At work. I played piano for a hotel in Sydney.'

'The Cove.'

'How did you know?'

Tahlia's brows rose in what Carissa could only interpret as surprise. 'Everyone who knows Ben…' She trailed off, thumbs working over her clipboard.

'We only met a couple of months ago,' Carissa said, and instantly felt the woman sizing her up.

'Then you'll already know he's got a heart as big as the outback,' Tahlia said. 'He took a chance on a girl he knew next to nothing about and arranged this job when I was down to my last dollar. There's nothing I wouldn't do for him.'

Carissa never doubted it. She smiled tightly. 'It's reassuring to know he inspires that kind of loyalty.'

'Believe it.' Tahlia met her eyes squarely for a moment before switching smoothly into business mode. 'I hope you're going to take advantage of all our facilities while you're here.'

'I'm going to try. It's a magnificent place, though, heaven knows, it must be costing Ben a small fortune.' She stopped, appalled at her gauche words.

Tahlia's hostess smile turned genuine, if enigmatic. 'Let him worry about that. Ah, here he comes now.' She rose, her clipboard in hand. 'Enjoy your stay, Carissa.' She turned and grinned at Ben, wagging an admonishing finger at him. 'Talk to your wife.'

What the blazes was that all about? Carissa wondered, her stomach tying itself into knots again. Ben and Ms Efficient with the trim body and neat hair had something going. She ran her fingers through her own damp, flyaway strands. Something Ben hadn't seen fit to clue her in on. She hadn't figured it out yet, but she would. Oh, yes, she would.

CHAPTER TEN

As BEN had promised, the little island beach was deserted, the sand white, the sea a clear aquamarine. Palm trees leaned over the beach, offering shade for their picnic. Carissa sat on the rug Ben had spread out and absorbed the tranquil beauty. The ribbons of sunlight rippling on the water, the emerald colour of the islands in the distance, the sea-scented warm breeze that played with her hair and slid over her body.

Ben opened the hamper and pulled out a sunny hibiscus, slid it behind her ear. 'You look like you belong to the islands.' He trailed his fingertips over her cheek, along her collar-bone beneath her tropical-print shirt. 'You want to move up here someday?'

She thought of Mel, her grandmother's house and the memories there. 'I love my home. I'd hate to leave it.'

'Then you'll never have to, Carissa. I promise you.'

She looked out to sea. But what of Ben? She couldn't allow herself—allow him—to get close, because unlike the way she'd been with Alasdair, she'd shatter when Ben left. Pieces of her heart were already breaking at the thought.

He poured a wine for himself, soda water for her, then raised his glass. 'To happy memories.'

She tapped her glass to his. 'Happy memories.' But she could barely swallow over the lump in her throat. Was that all she'd have one day?

Searching in the basket, Ben pulled out a carefully wrapped parcel tied with silver ribbon. 'This isn't standard issue,' he said, passing it to Carissa.

She passed it back. 'The card's for you.'

'Now I wonder how it got here? You got connections in the kitchen?' His eyes sparked with something Carissa imagined she might have seen in the face of the young boy Ben, and felt a tinge of regret that she wasn't responsible for putting the package there.

She remained silent, waiting while he took pleasure in the simple task of unwrapping it.

'A Christmas star?' She frowned. 'It's only April.'

'When you wish upon a star…' Ben held it up by its thread, spun it. It twinkled in the sunlight. 'It's from Tahlia. Actually, she's returning it. I gave it to her one Christmas.'

Tahlia. Again. That treacherous feeling stole through Carissa and this time she couldn't ignore it, or what it was. Jealousy. Ugly and foreign.

Alasdair had never inspired such feelings and she hated it, didn't know how to deal with it. She tossed back her soda water, planted her glass firmly on the rug and started to push up, with no idea what she intended to do.

'Whoa, there.' Ben grasped her hand. The spark remained in his eyes but his grin sobered. 'My blue lady's green.'

'What do you mean, green?' She tried to tug her hand away, with no luck.

'You know very well what I mean. And I like it.'

She shook her head and glared at the horizon. 'I sure as heck don't.'

'Sit down, Carissa.'

She did, because she knew he'd not let her go until he was good and ready.

'First off, there's nothing romantic between Tahlia and me.' Still keeping a grip, he stroked the inside of her wrist. Her pulse quickened. 'She's got a man in her life. Philip Conrad's the resort manager, and they're very happy.'

Carissa felt the heat rush to her face, suddenly ashamed of her behaviour. Pregnancy was making her feel vulnerable. 'You must be close, though. She knew you stayed at the Cove in Sydney.'

He turned away to gaze at the sea a moment. 'I haven't seen her in over a year, but she knows…because I own it.'

'You *own* the Cove Hotel. Own it.' Incredulous, she stared at him, then blew out a slow breath. 'I've worked there two years and you own it?'

His eyes twinkled back at her. 'Technically, I'm your employer. But only for the past few months. I signed the papers just before I left for the Desert Rock concert.'

'Why didn't you tell me?'

'You never asked.' His expression turned serious. 'You obviously weren't interested in what I did and I decided it was for the best. The less involved we were, the better for both of us.'

'But we are involved. We're married.' The words sounded foreign on her tongue. 'And I did ask you…in a roundabout sort of way. You never gave me a straight answer.'

'Could be because you asked in a roundabout way.' He leaned closer, stroking her hand again. 'I was going to tell you today. And while we're at it, the Black Opal Resort's mine too.'

'You own *luxury* hotels. No wonder Tahlia gave me a look. I was worried you were spending so much money—in your own hotel.'

He grinned. 'She'll be relieved you're concerned. And I didn't always travel first class. When my first employer died he left me a run-down pub west of Ceduna on the Nullabor Plain. It's taken fourteen years of bloody hard work to get where I am.'

Realisation hit. 'You rang Mr Christos. No wonder old Georgie was falling all over himself that morning. "Reconsidered", my foot.' She narrowed her eyes at him. 'I should be mad at you. You went behind my back and rang him after I expressly told you not to.'

Ben shook his head. 'I couldn't let you lose that job, sweetheart.'

Prepared to forgive, she said, 'Okay, I guess he was only following instructions. Stupid instructions, by the way. But he's still a jerk.'

'He's a dedicated employee,' he said, but chuckled nonetheless. 'Which came first, hotels or music?'

'I played after the pub closed for the night. There's not much to do at night in the middle of nowhere. I used to take my guitar into the desert and compose under the stars. When Rave hit the big time I wrote stuff for the band.'

At the mention of his friend his eyes clouded, the smile on his lips died. He opened the backpack he'd brought and pulled out a self-timing camera. 'I want something to remember our time here,' he said abruptly.

Sliding her sunglasses off, she watched him from the rug, the glints in his hair, the way the muscles in his forearms moved as he set the camera on a nearby rock and adjusted it.

'Coming ready or not.' In three quick strides he reached her, hugged her shoulders and they both smiled for posterity. 'Again.' And he was up, resetting the timer. 'Now.' Once more he fell on the rug beside her, scooting her body close.

After the camera whirred and clicked, he turned to look at her. She didn't want him to see the naked raw emotion she knew he'd see in her gaze and reached for her sunglasses.

'No.' He reached up and took her hat off. 'I want to see your eyes. Such a beautiful colour,' he murmured. 'They change with the surroundings. Right now they're as clear as the water and brimming with doubts.' His gaze dropped to her mouth, making it feel full and tingly. 'Kiss me. You've never initiated contact. It's always me making the moves.'

He leaned closer, till his face filled her vision, till his mouth was a soft sigh away from hers. Why should she deny him or herself the pleasure of a simple kiss? *Let go and live in the moment.*

She leaned in…and let go.

The world beyond them receded. The rustling palms, the waves lapping the shore faded to a blur of sound as her senses focused on him. Only him. His lips on hers, his breath on her cheek, the scent of tanning lotion and sun-warmed male skin. Heat drizzled through her body like liquid sunshine.

One hard palm reached behind her head, long fingers slid into her hair to massage the base of her skull and she almost groaned with pleasure. He'd always been gentle, but today she felt something deeper, hotter, simmering beneath the surface.

Her hands rose to cup his smooth, bare shoulders, fingertips absorbing the different textures as they drifted down over the hard planes of his chest, only to creep up again to caress the rough velvet jaw.

His free hand slid beneath her loose shirt and the thin swimsuit strap and his fingertips, callused from years of strumming guitar strings, had her melting with desire. Just the thought of those fingers skimming lower to tease her nipples, which hardened with anticipation, almost drove her over the edge.

Her mouth opened beneath his. Something urgent called to her, something primitive and frightening in its intensity. She could almost believe he felt something stronger, deeper than lust as his tongue danced over hers. Mindlessly her arms tightened around his neck, letting her breasts graze his chest through the layers of fabric.

When he pulled back a little to look at her, she almost whimpered with the loss.

'I want you.' His voice was low, rough with need. 'Naked and under me.'

The image of them tumbling over that king-size bed, skin to skin, male to female, sent a thrill racing through her body. Her gaze dropped to his firm abdomen with its sprinkling of dark hair, the flexing bulge beneath his shorts, and her pulse stepped up another notch. She wanted it too, but she wanted the sexual act *and* the man.

Dizzy with churning emotions, she weighed his words against the standards by which she'd lived her life. Wanting, lust was easily satisfied. It wasn't enough. She wanted—demanded—more of a life partner, the man she loved. She needed to be *needed*. For herself, not only for her body. She needed to be loved.

A man like Ben wouldn't understand. Heck, at this moment with her whole body craving completion, *she* didn't understand. She shook her head as she leaned away from him. 'Not here, not this way.'

'We can be back in our room in thirty minutes tops.'

'No. That's not what I mean.' She shook her head. 'There has to be more…' How could she explain that she needed something that went beyond a piece of paper that made it legal?

'Other than the fact that I'm your husband, and that kissing you feels damn good?' His voice was impatient, his breathing laboured and uneven.

'Yes.'

'Real life isn't a fairy tale. This is as real as it gets. You and me.' He splayed a warm, wide-palmed hand firmly over her belly. 'And our child.'

To cool the emotional intensity sizzling between them, she shifted so his hand fell away, and concentrated on the thin line of blue on the horizon.

He swore softly, harshly. With jerky movements he opened the beach umbrella, adjusting it so it shaded Carissa, then muttered, 'I need to cool off.'

He strode away, until he was waist-deep in the sea, then glanced over his shoulder. His bronzed body glistened in the sun. Frustration and something deeper burned like fire in his eyes.

She ached to call him back. To beg him to make love to her here on the sand beneath the blue sky with only the wind and palms to witness her capitulation. Then he turned seaward, dived beneath the surface.

Probably just as well. One day he'd walk away for good.

* * *

On their last day Ben blocked out an hour to go over the books. It was only a formality; he trusted Philip and Tahlia, but he wasn't likely to get a chance to come this way again for a while.

He shot off a few e-mails and sat back to watch the sky. Tropical thunderheads were building like ice-cream cones, purple and apricot. A perfect evening for lying in bed with a lover and listening to the rain.

For the past ten days he and Carissa had lazed on white beaches, hiked through rainforest, sipped drinks by the pool.

But the nights… He leaned back in his chair with a sigh of frustration. Soft and warm and wasted. Carissa had made it clear their marriage was for the sole purpose of raising their baby. She'd practically handed him a carte blanche to take any woman he wanted.

Not good for his ego. Probably his fault; he'd handled the whole proposal bit badly. He scrubbed a hand across his jaw, reminded himself he needed to shave. He didn't want another woman; he wanted Carissa. He wanted his wife.

Tomorrow they'd be home, and the real business of married life would set in. Carissa looked fragile right now, but he knew she wasn't. There was a strength in her, both physical and emotional. She'd handle it.

The first drum roll of thunder rumbled across the sky. Tonight. Tonight he'd end this self-imposed celibacy, barring Carissa's bouts of nausea, of course. She wasn't exactly falling all over him, but he guessed she was entitled to be temperamental. Still, it wouldn't hurt to throw in a candlelit dinner and soft music.

He shut down the computer, picked up the phone and prepared to call Room Service. It wasn't his area of expertise, but he could be romantic when the occasion called for it.

A cold meal of lobster, salads and fruit—so it wouldn't matter when they ate—lay beneath silver covers on a snowy tablecloth.

Four scented candles waited to be lit. Fresh frangipani floated in a crystal dish.

With everything organised, Ben kicked off his shoes, flicked on the TV and fell back onto the bed. He'd sent Carissa off for aromatherapy and a full body treatment with orders to the beautician to keep her there a while and make sure she relaxed.

Rain-scented air stirred beneath the slow turn of the overhead fan. The steady plop of water on the banana palm fronds by the patio soothed. He lowered the volume on the TV till it was a whitewash of sound, closed his eyes and drifted...

Blackness engulfed him, dragging him down to a bottomless pit. He was dreaming again and he couldn't wake. He struggled, knowing it was futile. The screeching sound of metal, the crackle of fire, choking smoke that seared his lungs, stung his eyes.

He tried to claw his way out, but his legs were lead pipes. He tried to call, but his throat was dry, filled with the taste of bile and the stench of burnt flesh. He could hear the roll of thunder and his own heart pounding its way out of his chest.

'Ben, Ben, wake up.' The voice of an angel, disembodied and calm. Hands, cool hands touching his flesh, dragging him up, pulling him out.

'Ben, what is it?'

He dragged in a gasp as if it were his last. A sweep of damp air chilled his sweat-slicked skin. It was still raining; the sweet smell of the rainforest wafted through the open patio doors.

He opened his eyes. The lamp in the corner had been switched on, the TV turned off. Carissa's face swam before him, eyes wide, dark with fear. *God, don't let her see me like this.* He turned his face into the pillow. 'Go away, Carissa.' Right now he wanted her more than life.

'I'm not going anywhere. Are you sick? I can't help you if you don't tell me.'

How could he tell her the horrors he dreamed? How sometimes life didn't offer second chances, how the world you thought you knew and the people you loved could vanish like lightning. 'I'm not sick. Leave me alone. You're not part of this. I won't let you be a part of this.'

'I'm your wife. I'm part of it whether you like it or not. If you're not ill, you were having one hell of a nightmare.'

Hell. 'Yeah.' She didn't know how close to the truth she was.

She turned his face until his vision was filled with her. Light fingers traced his brow, his cheek. Fresh from her beauty session, she smelled like heaven's garden, a place he had no business in. She didn't belong here with him.

'Ben, let me help.'

Her quiet words, the concern in those lovely eyes unmanned him. She unbelted her silky robe; it parted to reveal a glimpse of glowing skin. The swell of her breasts rose and fell with her breathing.

His stomach tightened at the implication. 'I don't need help.'

'You're not seeing you from where I'm standing.'

'You're not the only one who wants to be alone, Carissa.'

'Your response to that was to tell me I'm stubborn. And you were right.' Shucking the robe, she slipped onto the bed beside him. 'You try to shut me out and I'll just keep right on coming back.' She reached out with cool hands, cupped his tensed jaw in her palm.

He dragged her close until every gorgeous curve pressed against him. She went still but her eyes remained clear and steady on his. But his hands weren't steady as they moved over the cool, smooth skin of her hip. He could feel her heart thundering against his, matching his own erratic rhythm.

Blind need pumped through him. To touch and be touched, to be a part of life, and to be close to someone. Not just someone. Carissa. Not any willing body. Her body.

Her legs tangled with his as her arms slid around his neck. Then his mouth was on hers, hard and hungry, and he was lost in her. *Make me forget.*

Darkness, desperation, desire. He was aware of the sensations battering him, couldn't fight them as she drew his tongue against hers, traced circles on his nape with her fingertips. 'Need me,' she whispered. 'Need me now.' She arched and ground her belly against him, leaving him in no doubt about what she wanted.

Somehow he managed to shove down his boxers, then rolled on top of her. Her flesh was tight, hot, wet as he pushed himself inside. He heard her sharp indrawn breath, perhaps in shock, perhaps in pleasure, but she tightened her arms around his neck and he heard his own groan in response.

The faint but seductive sound of the sax and clarinet in the dining room mingled with the rhythmic patter of rain as he drove into her heat. He couldn't think, couldn't breathe, only knew that this was where he wanted to be. She made him feel whole, healed.

He kissed her neck and her body blossomed to life beneath him. The taste of her skin was like the sweetest tropical fruit, her scent as heady as the frangipani on the table.

All he could think was how much he wanted her, how much he needed her. She was his wife, the mother of his child, something he'd not realised he'd wanted. Until now.

Carissa gasped as his hot steel length plunged inside her with an urgency she'd never experienced. This was deep, dark and dangerous. Unleashed power tipping them both over the edge.

His mouth burned and branded, his hands raced over her breasts, cupping, moulding, squeezing, until she ached with the sweet torment. He was hot, strong, demanding, and her blood heated, her pulse raced in response. Knowing the child they'd made lay safely within her made her feel strong and all female; that it nestled between them now, something shared, drew her to him in a way she'd never imagined.

Weeks of wanting were forgotten. *Only wanting?* No, she thought dimly as she splayed her fingers over his back and felt the strong ripple of muscle, the thin film of sweat, this was so much more.

And then she couldn't think at all. He was like the sea, restless, relentless. Sensation after sensation rolled through her, endless waves of pleasure swamped her. But beneath that power his torment brewed.

'Take me with you.' She uttered the words against his shoulder, tumbled with him through the shadows, raced with him as he fought his demons.

Instinct had her matching his movements. Desperation had her clinging, sobbing. She arched with her body's shattering release, felt him come with a ferocity that both thrilled and shocked her.

She lay limp for a few moments, hearing the rain, feeling her blood pump, the sweat-dampened skin cool, Ben's weight on her body, his breath against her neck.

Too soon, he rolled off her and away with a harsh sound that spoke volumes.

She stared at the back of his head, the long, naked and muscular length of him. The sudden loss of that intimate contact chilled her; his terse sigh panicked her.

Every tingling nerve ending rebelled, every heavy thump of her heart was a reminder of what they'd shared. She couldn't ignore it, wouldn't. But obviously he didn't feel the same way. And why would he? An inexperienced woman wouldn't be enough for a man like Ben, used to females swooning at his feet, working their way into his bed.

Before she made a complete fool of herself she reached for her robe on the floor, dragged it on and sat on the edge of the bed. Damn him for making her doubt herself. There'd never been an obstacle she couldn't overcome until Ben Jamieson had charged his way into her life. Until she'd fallen in love with an impossible dream.

In the muted light she saw, for the first time, the intimate table, the flowers and candles. Anger drained away, replaced by heartache and misery.

She didn't even feel him slide across the bed until his hands closed gently over her shoulders. She jerked at the contact, but his hold tightened.

'Carissa. I'm sorry if I hurt you. You caught me at a bad moment. You were trying to help and I came at you like some un-civilised brute.' The sincerity of his apology glimmered in his eyes.

She didn't want apologies. She wanted something he couldn't give her. Rather than let him see the pain in her eyes, she focused them on the floor.

'Carissa, what happened tonight…'

'Was a healthy bout of sex,' she finished for him.

He turned her till she was facing him, tilted her chin. His eyes locked on hers, dark and deep and intense. 'Oh, sweetheart, it was so much more than that.'

A thrill raced through her at his words. Perhaps there *was* something there besides an apology. If so, she'd do whatever it took. 'I know you'll try to use your nightmares to stay away. It won't work. You have them often, don't you?'

'Have I disturbed you?'

'I've heard you on the porch, seen you pace the yard at night. I can't help you if you shut me out.'

'You don't know what you're getting yourself into,' he murmured into her hair, then tugged her down so they lay side by side facing each other.

'You let me worry about that.' She replayed his words in her head: *Sweetheart, it was so much more than that.* Her heart couldn't find its natural rhythm. It might be one small step in their relationship, but for the first time real hope hovered in her heart.

CHAPTER ELEVEN

CARISSA decided the best part about going away was coming home. But now 'home' came with a new set of complications. It wasn't only hers now, but a family home with this man she was still learning about, and, in a few months' time, a baby.

For the past few days she'd been living a dream. *Welcome back to reality.* The salty tang of Sydney's beaches, the call of wattle birds. The wait on the porch while someone other than her unlocked the door.

She was nervous—nervous about entering her own house, for heaven's sake. She stood beside him catching the smell of fresh paint as it wafted out the door, two almost-strangers not knowing how to play the moment.

'Wait here,' he said. She watched him walk down the hall, set her suitcase inside her room. Those nerves fluttered again—where did he intend putting his gear?

He motioned her forward. 'There've been a few changes. I hope you'll approve.'

As she approached his eyes remained on hers and she could've sworn he wasn't as confident as he'd like her to think. She stopped at the doorway and her breath caught in her throat.

The tired cream paint and faded wallpaper were gone. The walls radiated cool white. A dressing table and white wicker easy chair had replaced the scarred, garage-sale dresser and

kitchen chair. On the window sill a jug of daisies nodded in the
breeze. A large rug in muted blues partially covered polished
floorboards.

Then there was the Bed, a white wrought-iron production
with a sapphire spread that flowed to for ever. 'Oh…'

'Mel helped,' he said, seeing Carissa stumped for words. 'She
knows what you like, so I thought…'

'It's gorgeous.'

'I wanted you to be comfortable while you're pregnant.' He
moved to the bed, pressed the mattress and nodded. 'Firm but
not too firm.'

And big enough to get lost in. She could imagine Ben
stretched out between the sheets. She wouldn't get lost if he was
there to hold her.

Was she still living the dream? All the way home she'd relived
last night's passion. How he'd clung to her as if she were a
lifeline, their frantic coupling in the dead of night. *Oh, sweetheart, it was so much more than that.* Did this makeover and
beautiful bed mean he intended to sleep with her now that the
honeymoon was over?

'You must be tired. You barely got three hours' sleep last
night.' His voice turned a trifle husky on the last two words, and
her pulse picked up, but before she could think about, let alone
voice an improper suggestion, he said, 'Why don't you stretch
out and take a nap?'

You. Meaning alone—not precisely what she'd had in mind.
So much for improper suggestions. Ben himself showed no sign
of sleep deprivation, just the stubble and a slightly tousled look.
Didn't mean she couldn't entice him to join her…

Except, she'd never seduced a man. Correction: until last
night she'd never seduced a man. Her blood heated at the
memory. Had that aggressive woman who'd refused food for
another bout between the sheets really been her?

Now, in her own surroundings, in stark daylight, those old insecurities pressed in on her. He was used to experienced women; last night he'd needed someone, an entirely different scenario. Today he was back in control.

'I will.' Her heart beating hard, she focused her eyes on his and moved towards him. 'In a little while.'

He slid his arms around her waist and pressed a kiss to her temple. His heat seeped through her clothes, his masculine soap smell filled her nose. His hands on her lower back were soothing. But impersonal. He wasn't the desperate lover who'd taken her on that wild ride to heaven in the small hours of this morning.

That lover would have dispensed with clothes at the front door. He'd have had her up against the wall, spread-eagled before him while he did wicked things to her with his hands and tongue and teeth. And that hard wedge of masculine flesh she could feel poking into her belly despite his cool outward control would have been—

The sound of the front door opening had her jerking guiltily out of his arms. Her skin was tingling and the heat in her cheeks had spread through her body and throbbed dangerously between her thighs. She couldn't look at Ben.

'Hello?' Mel's voice drifted down the passage.

'In here, Mel.' With unsteady fingers Carissa adjusted her blouse, then laughed, still visualising the scene her stepsister *hadn't* walked in on.

'What?' she heard Ben say, but she was already halfway down the hall.

'Hi.' Mel hugged her, then grinned when she saw Ben leaning against the bedroom door, those wicked, *innocent* hands now in his pockets. 'Whoops, I guess I interrupted something.'

'No. I was being coaxed into a nap,' Carissa began, then realised how Mel would interpret that.

'Sounds like fun.' Mel's grin widened. 'I didn't expect you back for another hour. I wanted to drop a few things off before I go to work.' She picked up the grocery bag she'd brought. 'I'll put this in the kitchen and leave you lovebirds to get on with your...nap.'

Ben took the groceries from Mel. 'Carissa wanted to come home a couple of hours earlier. I'll let you two catch up while I take the car for a spin.'

Mel sighed as he disappeared into the kitchen. 'Cute backside.'

'So you've said, more than once.'

'Cute everything. Who'd have thought Ben Jamieson'd be such a marshmallow?'

'Who'd have thought.'

'Is that a hint of possessiveness I hear in your voice? Don't worry, for all his charm, he's not my type. Come on. Into the living room. I want the latest.'

'Thanks for all you've done here.' Carissa indicated the renovated room. 'I can see your hand in this. And the bedroom's gorgeous.'

'And if I'd stayed away you'd have christened the bed by now.'

Carissa wasn't so sure. At the sound of the Porsche purring down the drive, Mel pulled Carissa onto the couch. 'So tell me all about it. Well—not *all*. Skip the scenery and get to the juicy parts.'

'Mel,' Carissa scolded in a strangled voice. 'A honeymoon's private.'

'Okay. I guess I'll settle for the scenery.'

'The resort's something out of this world.'

'And how did you two get on? Apart from the s-e-x, I mean.'

'Okay, mostly.'

'Mostly?'

Carissa thought of the brooding side of Ben, the hurting that haunted him. 'Sometimes he's hard to reach. I want to get him interested in music again. He seems determined to shut that part of his life away.'

'Well, that segues perfectly into the other item I wanted to talk to you about. You're looking at the hospital's newly elected president of the Rainbow Road.'

'For the kids with cancer?'

Mel nodded. 'I'm organising a fun afternoon in June. Music, magicians, that kind of thing. I'd like you to play for them.'

'Sure.'

'We'll set up in the common room, there's a piano there, and if you can bring your guitar—it's more intimate with kids— nursery rhymes for the littlies and something more upbeat for the older ones.'

And just what Ben needed, Carissa thought. 'I'll bring Ben, it'll be good for him. Put us both down.'

'You don't want to check with him first?'

'No, he'll be there, but don't tell him yet. When he sees those kids he won't be able to say no.'

Carissa popped the honey biscuits she was making for the kids' afternoon into the oven, then wandered to the window to watch the resident gardener at work.

Scarlet and gold leaves littered the lawn, the trees were all but bare, but today he was installing a sprinkler system. Perhaps it was an odd activity to herald winter, but he seemed to find pleasure and solace in her garden. And it *was* a garden now—he had a surprisingly green thumb and she was more than happy to pass on the responsibility.

He squatted, his old T-shirt riding up his spine, jeans low at his back, revealing a patch of bare, tanned skin and a nice handful of backside.

She smiled, remembering how tight and warm it had felt beneath her hands in bed this morning. An almost-perfect lover. Her smile faded a little. In her books 'lover' implied 'love'. But Ben had never promised her love. The word had been absent from their marriage vows, nor had he ever spoken that word to her.

But they had an open and honest relationship—even if this afternoon's concert was a secret she hadn't told him about. During the day both were busy with work, but the nights… She sighed. She couldn't have wished for a more caring and gentle man.

And watching him wasn't getting the weekend chores done. It was getting harder holding down two jobs and making a home. She knew she could have chucked in waitressing any time and taken on an extra piano gig, but she had something to prove to herself.

It was a matter of pride and independence that she could stand on her own feet, even if those feet ached most of the time. If Ben left she needed to know she could.

She'd give waitressing one more month. By then she'd be five months along. Time then to hang up her apron and concentrate on herself and her baby.

She'd given strict orders that the room she'd earmarked for the nursery was off limits. She wanted the pleasure of doing the whole job herself, right down to painting the walls and hanging the curtains, although Ben hadn't agreed to letting her do anything requiring a ladder.

The little froth and bubble ripple fluttered deep inside her. She pressed a hand to her abdomen, held her breath. Again. The baby was moving. That tiny fragile life was saying, *I'm not ready to face the world yet, but I'm here.* Tears welled up and over. The rush of love, for her child, for the man who'd put it there, swamped her, leaving her shaken with its depth. And she wanted to share it.

Ben inserted the last dripper into the tubing he'd laid and stood back to view his achievements. A chill wind cooled the sweat on his brow as he turned on the tap and adjusted the water flow. Crazy time of year to put in a sprinkler system, he decided, but why not? Carissa seemed so anxious for him to do it now, while the ground was soft.

After the hard years of building a business reputation he could be proud of and the even crazier world of music, the peace and comfort here was a kind of therapy. Besides, he wanted the place finished before the baby came.

The thought that he might not be here come summer to see the garden in its full glory intruded into his mind like a rose thorn. No. He glared at the garden he'd resurrected. He'd be here. Damned if he wouldn't. But his father's words hammered at him. *The only thing you're good at is running away.*

And wasn't that the ultimate irony? Good old Dad had faced his problems by putting a bullet through his head with his cop's firearm. In the end he'd done his wife a favour. She no longer had to put up with the abuse he'd thrown at her for as long as Ben could remember.

It had destroyed her.

Ben wrenched the tap off and strode to the shed for the rake. He had a chance at something worthwhile here. This was his family now and he was staying. Anger and determination continued to push through him as he began to rake the leaves into piles.

The back screen door squeaked open, slammed shut. He looked up and saw Carissa on the top step and his dark mood lifted. She had a strange expression on her face, as if she was focusing inward. Pregnancy had rounded and softened her curves, but it hadn't diminished her sexuality, or his desire. The sky was dark, threatening rain, yet her cheeks glowed with the look of spring.

Their eyes met. The wind chased over the yard, scattering the leaves he'd raked and pressing his red plaid flannel shirt she wore against her body. Something deep and unfamiliar plunged through him. He felt as if he'd been tossed high, then dumped by a tidal wave. His pulse scrambled as he fought the feeling; his body tensed as his loins grew heavy. He couldn't move. Like some kind of idiot he could only stand and stare as if he'd never seen a pregnant woman before. *His* pregnant woman, carrying *his* baby.

'Ben?'

He jerked out of his thrall. 'What? Is something wrong?' The words came out harsh, clipped, as he fought the whip of panic.

'No. Everything's fine,' she assured him as she drew close. Her face was radiant, beautiful. 'The baby moved.'

Again that strange sensation rolled over him. 'Are you sure?'

'I'm sure. Here.' She hesitated, then reached out, took his hand, placed it on her belly.

Apart from lovemaking, he'd avoided conscious touching as her stomach swelled. It was one way to keep an emotional distance, not to let himself give in to the growing need he had to be with her, to be near her.

So he was as surprised as she when his hand moved under hers. 'Jeez...' His throat was thick, choked. He was touching his child. He splayed his fingers wider over the hardness and met her gaze.

She was smiling back at him, a deep, tender smile he'd never seen before. It made him weak at the knees.

He frowned. 'I don't feel anything.'

'Perhaps it's too early for anyone else to feel yet.'

'Yeah.' But his hand remained, wanting that connection a little longer.

Keeping his eyes on hers, he found himself inching up the flannel. He saw her quick intake of breath, and his own quickened in response. His fingers connected with warm, bare flesh. She was round and ripe, and all woman.

His other hand rose to cup the small mound between his palms. He dropped to his knees to see what he was touching. Her hands smelled of honey and spice as she threaded her fingers though his hair, reminding him of his childhood when his mother had baked.

It hit him like a bolt of lightning, as powerful as it was terrifying. He needed her and this baby more than he needed to breathe. This baby bound them together for ever. They'd always be a part of each other's lives.

Reeling, he dropped his hands. His whole body was on fire. The need to feel that baby against his own naked belly was like a molten storm in his veins. 'Come to bed.'

She shook her head, but she was smiling. 'We're going to be late to the hospital. The Rainbow Road's kids' concert, remember?'

He shoved a frustrated hand through his hair and ordered his body to cool off. 'Yeah.' Carissa wouldn't let those kids down. He was learning that his wife always put others' needs before her own. In this case those kids won hands down over his healthy libido. 'Guess I'll go take a shower.' A very cold shower.

But tonight… Tonight he was going to keep her hot, naked and close.

Ben parked the Porsche in the hospital's underground car park.

'Can you get my guitar?' Carissa asked as she climbed out.

He glanced behind him at the back seat. 'I didn't see you put that in. When did you learn guitar?'

'At school. I'm no pro but I get by.' Her fingers were restless, tapping a staccato on the music folder she was hugging to her chest. If he wasn't mistaken, she appeared edgy. Or was it excitement? She seemed high on energy. Surely she wasn't a nervous performer.

They walked to the elevator, her shoes making a quick tapping sound on the concrete. Inside the lift, she pressed the third-floor button, then leaned against the wall, watching the floor numbers light up.

As the elevator dinged and the doors whooshed open she turned to him, eyes dancing with anticipation. 'Ben…never mind.' Pushing away from the wall before he could ask her what she meant, she stepped out.

The banner strung across the double doors to the common room told him all he needed to know.

'The Rainbow Road welcomes Ben Jamieson, songwriter and guitarist.'

Something like a fist slammed into his gut and crawled up his throat. His hands, suddenly ice-cold, tightened on Carissa's guitar case. 'What the…?' His gaze cut to her and he knew he'd been set up. Set up by the one person who should have understood.

'Ben…' That sparkling excitement in her eyes died, replaced by uncertainty. She took a step towards him, one hand outstretched, must have thought better of it and stopped. 'I thought—'

But he cut her off with a slash of his hand. Anger was preferable to the icy fear that chilled his blood, the cold sweat breaking out on his body. '*You* thought? You thought wrong.'

The spectre of his nightmare, of Rave's dead eyes, rose up before him. He hid his shudder by doing a sharp about-turn and paced away.

All you're good at is running away.

'They're expecting you. I'm counting on you.' Her softly spoken words cut through his defences. He turned, every muscle in his body screaming to get the hell out before she saw what a coward he was. The rosy bloom in her cheeks had vanished. Beneath the jeans and loose blue shirt with its rainbow embroidery she was trembling. But she lifted her chin. 'I wanted you to pick up music again.'

'So you went behind my back and expect me to perform like your trick dog? I told you I wasn't ready.'

'You never will be if you don't start. If you can't do this one thing for me, do it for the kids. Do it for yourself.'

The doors opened and a stick-thin boy of about seven came out in hospital pyjamas. His skin was a waxy shade of pale.

'Hi, Miss Grace.'

Carissa cast a meaningful but sad glance at Ben before she smiled. 'Hello, Zac, how's it going?' She turned back to Ben. 'Your guitar's in the common room. I found it in your studio and had Mel bring it. I'm going in now. She'll wonder where we are.' She pushed through the doors, leaving her delicate scent to mingle with the antiseptic smell in the austere linoleum-covered corridor. And one sick boy.

Zac's eyes widened. 'Hey, you're Ben Jamieson! I listen to your music. XLRock's totally cool.'

Ben forced a smile. 'Thank you, but I don't… Why aren't you inside with the others?'

'Clowns are for kids. I was waiting for Ben Jamieson.'

'Well, you found him.'

'Can you teach me to play like you?' He nodded towards Carissa's guitar he'd forgotten he was clutching.

On the other side of the doors he could hear a clown's squeaky horn and kids laughing.

'Let's see your fingers.' He took Zac's hands, felt their fragility and something squeezed in his chest, but he said, 'Yep, they'll do the job. Come here.' Then he sat down on a nearby hospital bench, drew out the guitar and began tuning it.

'You'll have to teach me quick because I'm not well.' Zac's plain statement of fact, spoken without emotion, made Ben want to weep. His fingers tightened on the guitar. It was time to start living again.

'Mr Jamieson?' Zac tugged on his arm.

'Call me Ben,' he told him, slinging the strap over the boy's shoulders. He guided Zac's fingers to the strings. 'Let's see how we go here.'

Carissa silently thanked Zac for his timely interruption as she pushed through the doors. Fortunately the doors were at the back of the audience. It gave her a moment to pull herself together.

She'd made a big mistake not telling him. Huge. Music was a trigger for all those bad memories, the guilt, the nightmares. Why hadn't she realised that? A rising nausea wrenched at her stomach, clutched her by the throat, making it almost impossible to breathe.

His issues went so much deeper than she'd thought. Anyone with half a brain who saw him suffer in the dead of night would see it. Sweating, calling out in his sleep, twisting the covers off until he stole silently from their bed to sleep alone on the couch, or wander the yard.

She fought the cold sweat that broke out on her body and leaned against the doors, dragging in air. She'd allowed him to walk that yard alone, to sleep alone on the couch, to deal with his pain. Alone. *Stupid, stupid, stupid.* Hadn't she promised support and understanding when she'd made her marriage vows? Ben had upheld his end of the bargain.

The clown finished his act with a flurry of gold dust, which he showered over the kids. Then Mel saw her and she was out of time.

Plastering a smile on her face, she pushed forward, giving light-hearted high fives to the kids as she went. But she felt as if she were walking through quicksand.

'Where's Ben?' Mel whispered.

'In the corridor with Zac.' Swallowing over her dust-dry throat, she whispered, 'It's just me for now.' She turned and waved at her audience. 'Hi, everyone. Ready for some music?' She sat down at the piano and launched into a bracket of children's favourites while Mel handed out percussion instruments for them to tap along.

The round of applause signalled the next act.

Ben.

The baby chose that moment to kick, a heart-rending reminder of this morning when he'd kissed her naked belly, his expression of wonder and something deeper... Her chest grew impossibly tight, so tight she bit her lip against the pain.

Melanie lifted her shoulders in question.

'Where's Ben Jamieson?' someone asked.

Carissa took a steadying breath and prepared to stand, to disappoint a bunch of kids. And herself. 'Mr Jamieson is...' She looked helplessly towards the door.

Ben stood just inside with an adoring Zac beside him. Her heart stood still as his eyes locked with hers. She wanted to think it was forgiveness she saw in the dark intensity of their depths, an acknowledgement that in her own misguided way she'd tried to help. But in that split second across a room alive with noise and kids and balloons she couldn't be sure.

He nodded, a barely discernable movement. 'Right here.'

Her vision blurred with unshed tears. 'Let's give him a Rainbow Road welcome.'

Carissa knew nothing about Ben Jamieson the songwriter, the entertainer. This wasn't the same man who shared her bed and left the toothpaste uncapped on her vanity.

This man kept his young audience entertained with songs they could join in; he let Zac and a few other children try out his guitar. He had a natural rapport with kids. He flirted with the female nurses—he also had a natural rapport with women.

At the close of his performance he asked Carissa to join him with her guitar. He hugged her to his side and told the kids she was his wife. As if he was proud of her. As if he loved her. No one would have suspected those angry and heart-wrenching moments on the other side of the door.

But as soon as the performance finished, he took off. When she and Mel had finished tidying up, Mel dropped her home. Then she found the note on the bed. 'If you need anything, leave a message on my mobile.'

'I need *you*, Ben. Only you.' Sinking onto the bed, Carissa hugged his pillow, breathing in his scent and wishing with all the love in her heart that it could've ended differently. Because she had a feeling it was never going to be the same between them ever again.

CHAPTER TWELVE

BEN punched down on the accelerator as a rainstorm rolled in over Sydney harbour. He wanted the speed, the feel of power beneath his hands, the sound of the engine's purr. He had a measure of control over his car even if he didn't have it over his wife or his feelings.

The wipers thwacked over the windscreen, light bounced off the wet, windswept road as the evening closed in. He turned on the demister and lowered the window as the glass fogged, letting in exhaust fumes and the hiss of tyres on water, and worked his way through traffic and out of the city.

Carissa would be home by now. The thought sent a jolt of guilt through him. He didn't want to hurt her. But today she'd seen more than he'd been willing to show her. His hands tightened on the wheel. Worse, she'd held up a mirror so he'd had no choice but to take a good look at himself and he hadn't liked what he'd seen.

Which made him think about what he'd seen in Carissa today. She'd had faith in him; she'd believed in him. And earlier he'd held his unborn child between his hands. So she was stubborn; she also had strength and was fair to boot. She was also sexy as hell, and a goddess in bed.

He felt the familiar quick, deep clutch at his groin. The one he always felt when he thought of Carissa naked and glorious, her hair silky against his body, her lips soft and full on his skin.

It wasn't just the sex. He'd had more than his share of faceless women with perfect, athletic and silicone bodies, quick, hot, frantic couplings that left his body satisfied and his soul empty.

With Carissa it was so much more. The thought, quite frankly, terrified him. Shaking it away, he straightened, rolled his shoulders and concentrated on the road. He had some long hours' driving ahead.

Before he saw Carissa again he had to tell someone he should have told a long time ago.

The Arches Rest Home was a turn-of-the-century blue-stone structure in Melbourne's leafy eastern suburbs. Care cost an arm and a leg, but the place was immaculate. A sea of lawn flowed gently to a perimeter of oaks, the last brown leaves fluttering in the watery morning sun.

Security demanded he check in at the front desk before heading to his mother's room. Light from a huge arched window limned the high-backed armchair where his mother spent her days. Soft chamber music drifted from the CD player he'd had installed for her.

'How's she been?' he asked the nurse who'd accompanied him.

'The same. She's comfortable.' She moved to the window, flicked the curtain wider. 'You've a visitor, Mrs Jamieson.'

Ben rounded the chair. 'Hello, Mum.' He kissed her cheek, smelled the subtle fragrance of the expensive soap he'd left her last time. She looked the same as she had last month. Lost.

She had a pretty face, but her eyes, so like his own, were vacant. Her short hair was carefully combed, her loose green dress clean and ironed.

'Can I get you something to drink, Mr Jamieson?' the nurse asked at the doorway.

'Thanks, no.'

'I'll be at the desk if you need me.'

'How've you been, Mum? You're as beautiful as ever.' He stroked her hand, willing her to come back, if only for a moment, so he could tell her what was in his heart. His jaw tightened. This was almost worse than death. You could grieve over a death and move on.

He increased his pressure on her hand. 'Mum, I've got some news. You're going to be a grandmother. Did you hear me, Mum? A grandma. Carissa—that's my wife's name—I haven't told you that either, have I? She's a wonderful pianist. You'd love her music…

'Next time I'll bring Carissa and let you hear for yourself. Would you like that? Beautiful music—Beethoven and stuff. She's strong and smart and caring.' *And I don't deserve her.*

Somewhere down the hall a vacuum cleaner hummed, dishes rattled. Another day like the last. An endless string of days his mother wasn't aware of. Her life was slipping away, wasted, and it damn near broke his heart. Now that she could live the life she deserved, had earned, and she couldn't even feed herself.

'Mum…' He broke off. He found he couldn't say what was in his heart after all, because he couldn't acknowledge it aloud, not even to himself.

He *cared* for Carissa, dammit, and knew she cared for him. They had a good relationship barring a few wrinkles which could be ironed out. They fitted well together. In some things they were miles apart, totally in sync in others. He wanted her, in bed and out. If he needed her, she needed him back. Partners, a duo act.

'Mum…' he began again. 'We have a chance to be a family. I want you to be a part of that family too. I want to see you bounce our kid on your knee and sing those crazy kid rhymes you used to sing to me.'

He barely noticed the way his voice had softened, the way his hand tightened over hers. He was too aware of the pain that gripped his heart. 'A family, Mum. The way we used to be before it all went wrong. Wake up, Mum, and you can come live with us—there's plenty of room.' His voice broke. *'Come back.'*

She continued to stare beyond the window at something only she could see.

'Mr Jamieson? Are you okay?'

He felt the nurse's hand on his shoulder and realised his eyes were watering. 'Been driving for hours,' he muttered. He pulled himself up off his knees, pressed a last kiss to his mother's cheek. 'I'll be back.'

He'd reached the door when he heard the words that stopped him in his tracks.

'She's in your heart.'

Pulse thundering in his ears, he turned slowly. Retraced his steps. His mother's eyes were still vacant, her hand resting on her lap as he'd left it. But he'd heard her voice. A voice he hadn't heard in ten years.

Carissa lifted the kitchen curtain and told herself it was for the last time. Outside was dark and still, a few stars twinkled between the clouds. She shivered and snuggled deeper into Ben's flannel shirt, breathing in his scent. She'd rolled up the sleeves, but the fabric stretched across her middle.

Ben hadn't answered her message to let her know where he was and if he was all right. There was nothing she could do but wait. The guilt and helplessness were a gnawing pain eating away at her soul. Her fingers twisted in the curtain's fabric. Obviously he wasn't coming home tonight.

The past thirty hours had been pure torture. She didn't know if he'd had an accident, where he was or who he was with, or if he was ever coming back. If he'd been here she'd have reached out to him, told him how sorry she was and asked him to make love with her. No, begged, if that was what it took.

As she paced she tried to bring his face to mind, but all she could see was his white-lipped anger when he'd told her he wasn't ready.

And still he'd performed. Because she'd asked him to. And

only she would have seen the emotion behind that clever mask when he'd picked up his guitar and strummed that first chord.

On a sob of frustration, she slammed her palm on the table, then marched to her bedroom. There was nothing left to do but go to bed and try to sleep. Pacing the floor and worrying wasn't doing her or the baby any good and she had to work tomorrow afternoon.

A hot shower would ease the tension. She shivered as she stripped down and tied up her hair, then sighed as she slid under its soothing spray. As she reached for the shower gel she felt a draught of air, saw the blur of movement through the fogged glass.

For what seemed like an eternity everything inside her froze. Hardly daring to move, she closed her fingers over the long-handled back scrub, then, with her heart tripping double time, reached towards the glass door, her feeble weapon raised.

Before she could get her stiff fingers to work, the door slid open with a smooth slide of metal on metal.

'You want me to help you with that?' The familiar smoky voice slid through her muddled senses.

'Oh... Ben.' She sobbed out his name as relief poured through her.

He stood on the fluffy white bath mat while steam gushed out and water spattered his jeans and sneakers. He hadn't shaved, his eyes were bloodshot and shadowed with fatigue.

It was the most beautiful sight she'd ever seen.

'Oh, yes. Please...'

He took the brush from her limp hand and turned her around, then stepped in behind her.

Her whole body went weak. She felt as if she were dissolving like jelly in the rain. Mingling with the spray, the scent of leather upholstery and male sweat surrounded her like a warm mist. His breath was a hot pool of air on her nape.

He slid the brush from neck to buttocks in one slow pass. Every bristle was an exquisite pinprick of pleasure as he slid it over her shoulder, along her collar-bone. *More.*

The brush dropped to the floor with a clatter as he turned her to face him. His T-shirt was plastered to his skin, his nipples dark against the fabric.

'You came back.' She heard the slightly hysterical edge to her voice as she raised her eyes to his.

Desire met desire, his nostrils flared, but his mouth remained grim, his jaw rock-hard and unforgiving. Like the ridge she felt against her swollen belly as he shifted his squelching runners in the tiny cubicle.

'Did you think I wouldn't?' Without taking his eyes off hers he toed off his sodden shoes, peeled off his socks. Dragged the shirt over his head and tossed it down. It hit the floor with a wet slap. A loud, impatient, needy sound.

'I tried *not* to think.' Her hands were on his flesh. His stomach was hard, lean, ridged with muscle. Water cascaded over his chest, catching on the masculine hair and running in rivulets into his waistband.

His eyes darkened and the bulge below his waist jerked against her, but his hands remained at his sides. 'Then you don't know me, Carissa. You don't know me at all.'

Carissa willed away the sting and concentrated on the difficult job of working the top button of his sodden jeans. 'I want to know you, Ben.' Her hands trembled as she tried to tug denim and briefs down over his hips as one.

His hands moved as if to push her away, but she looked into his passion-filled eyes and shook her head. 'All of you.'

Finally she managed to shove the offending garments down far enough so that her hands closed over his hard, silky length.

He jerked, his elbow colliding with the tap. 'Hell, Carissa…'

'Let me. We've got plenty of time. It's two showers for the price of one.'

She watched his face contort as if in pain as she dropped to her knees and he realised her intention.

'Carissa…' he warned, his voice hoarse.

'Shut up, Ben.' The soft skin at the top of his thighs begged for her lips, but she resisted for the moment to take in his mile-long, hairy legs as she shoved his jeans the rest of the way to the floor.

She batted his hands away when he would have pulled her up. While the water ran over their bodies, she kissed her way up one leg, lingered over the smooth skin of his groin.

She cupped the heavy weight of his testicles, squeezing gently, massaging the base of his thick arousal with her thumbs. On a groan he jerked beneath her fingers and fisted his hands in her hair. Encouraged, she lowered her head, swirled her tongue over the tip.

'Enough,' he rasped. He tugged her up his body, the slippery slide of flesh against flesh.

Steam rose around them, enclosing them in a cocoon of intimacy, shutting the world and its problems out. He reached for the shower gel, poured a generous dollop onto a palm and rubbed them slowly together.

The first touch of his hands on her breasts had the blood pulsing beneath her skin, her nipples contracting until they were tight little points of desire.

Weak with wanting, she leaned against the tiles for support. Her head fell back, exposing her throat for his hungry mouth. She felt boneless, as if she just might slide down the wall into a puddle of pure bliss.

While he lapped at her neck, his hands glided lower, over her swollen belly in slow, slippery circles, then lower still, till he found the place that ached for his touch.

'I want you.' His voice was harsh and filled with need. Joy flooded her as he slid one finger inside her, sending her pulse sky-rocketing. 'Tell me you want me.'

'I want you, Ben Jamieson. I've never wanted anything or anyone more than I want you.'

His body was hot, the tiles cool and smooth as he pressed his body against hers, drawing her hands over her head. Intense eyes, shifting from jade to midnight, watched her as his mood darkened, deepened. 'You're mine,' he said, and pushed inside her.

She met his gaze. 'That makes *you* mine.'

Her words seemed to have an instant effect on him. His grip tightened, and something raw and primitive crossed his expression. She'd never seen that look before and it drew a similar response from her, like some sort of mating call, both thrilling and terrifying. She felt bound, owned.

She matched him stroke for stroke as she yielded to him, sagging against the wall, only prevented from falling by his grasp on her wrists. She arched as he drove her up, up and over, then he spilled inside her with a sigh that seemed to come from the depths of his soul.

For a moment Ben buried his face against her neck and held her, knowing she'd slide away. Her full breasts and hard belly pressed against him. A fierce protectiveness welled up. He wanted to stay close like this a little longer, but lack of sleep was taking its toll. Dammit. Reluctantly he let her hands go, and she rolled her shoulders, rubbed her wrists.

He took over that task himself. 'Did I hurt you?'

'No.' She pressed a kiss to his chin. 'But if I don't get out of here I'm going to turn into a prune.'

She'd lightened the moment deliberately, he guessed, but he felt a twinge of disappointment. The powerful emotions wrung from the past few moments deserved more. He had to work to match her tone. 'I'm very partial to prunes.'

He nibbled at her neck, breathing in the fragrance of her flushed skin. Shut off the water. Then he handed her a towel and patted himself dry.

She reached past him for the hairdryer. 'Will you wait for me?' She sounded casual, but her eyes were vulnerable.

'I'll be waiting.' He strolled naked into the bedroom, turned back the cover and slid between the cold, crisp sheets.

He was exhausted, but all he could think about was her fierce declaration. *That makes you mine.* Warmth glowed through his body. On the first day of their marriage she'd all but given him a carte blanche to take any woman he wanted. She didn't know how badly he wanted it to work between them.

He hadn't looked at another woman since the first night he'd seen her. He hadn't known then that pleasure could be so inextricably bound up with pain, that need could be so sharp that it pierced the soul and left you weak…

He stirred to reluctant wakefulness as Carissa shifted beside him, her legs twining with his. God, what time was it? He glanced at the clock. 6:00 a.m.

Grey light softened the darkness, enough to see the dim oval of her face. And her wide eyes watching him. He reached out to touch the soft curve of her jaw, traced the slim column of her throat. 'Sorry.'

'You fell asleep the moment you hit the bed.' Her tone was faintly accusatory.

'I drove to Melbourne. To see my mother. Guess the shower did me in.'

Her eyes glittered with awareness, but she remained silent a moment as if weighing the truth of his words. 'So how was she?' she said at last.

'The same. No…' He hesitated. 'She said something—at least I thought she did. I spoke to the doctor about it and he looked her over, did a couple of tests. There's no change. He said that happens sometimes. It doesn't mean she's getting better.'

Carissa propped her head on a hand, eyes warm and understanding. 'What did she say?'

He shook his head. 'I didn't catch it,' he lied. He couldn't tell her, not yet, but someday…

She leaned over and took his hand, pressed it to her porcelain-smooth cheek. 'I'm so sorry for that. Are you going to take me to visit sometime? I want to meet this incredible woman who raised such a wonderful son.'

The way she looked at him—tender, warm, compassionate… He swore the sky brightened a little faster at that moment, bringing the rose of dawn to her cheeks. 'We'll go soon,' he promised.

Stress and overwork and finally grief had led to his mother's current state. He wasn't going to let it happen to Carissa. Starting now. 'I know you want your independence but there'll be no more working at the Three Steps.'

To his surprise she didn't bristle at his no-negotiation. In fact she smiled. 'I made a deal with myself, that if you came back I'd give up work and make a home for us.' She hesitated. 'If that's what you want.'

'I want.' The glow inside him grew and spread until it pulsed like fire, and his hand moved to her breast where he could feel her heart, matching the rhythm of his own. 'I wasn't prepared for the hospital gig and I just plain lost it. Nothing else has changed.'

'And I should've asked you first.'

'Maybe it's best you didn't.' He leaned up on his elbow, wanting to forget the last few days. 'We'll shop for nursery furniture today. I saw this great wooden rocking-horse…it's not too early, is it?'

He saw her lips curve in the semi-darkness. 'It'll be a while before we get to the rocking-horse stage. But that doesn't matter. Let's go get a rocking-horse.' She snuggled into him and closed her eyes. 'After lunch.'

He scooted her closer, pressed a kiss to her brow. Life meant something again. He was standing on the cusp of something so huge, so powerful it threatened to overwhelm him. She gave him hope when he'd forgotten what hope was. His mother was no longer able to, but Carissa reminded him how it felt to have someone care enough to worry when you didn't come home.

Somehow this woman had brought healing and closure to the darkest months in his life, and for the first time since Rave's death, he truly felt he'd make it.

* * *

Carissa stood in the centre of the room they'd chosen for the nursery and turned a slow circle. She hugged the framed picture of a white unicorn they'd bought yesterday while the hand-painted rocking-horse waited for its young rider in the corner.

A protective sheet covered the most adorable cradle she'd ever seen and a cute teddy night-light sat on the chest of drawers. She'd unearthed her grandmother's rocking-chair from the store room, stripped and lacquered it till its original wood gleamed.

Ben had gone to the Cove for a staff meeting and to meet with an architect about some renovations. Then he was going by the hospital to give Zac another guitar lesson.

She smiled to herself as happiness sparkled through her. At last he'd begun to heal. To look beyond his immediate surroundings and take those first steps towards a new life. If she could be patient a little longer, her dreams of a home filled with love and laughter and a husband who returned that love might not be out of reach. There'd be more kids, a dog with floppy ears and big feet, a cat or two.

Propping the print against the wall, she dragged the ladder across the scarred wooden floorboards, then grabbed the hammer and picture hook.

Then she remembered. Ben had absolutely forbidden her to climb the ladder. He'd insisted on painting the upper half of the walls himself. He'd also promised to hang the print last night because she couldn't wait to see how it looked, but they'd gotten seriously sidetracked on the new Persian rug. Then he'd promised faithfully to hang it before he left this morning, but he'd forgotten—they'd gotten sidetracked again.

Well, she was pregnant, not disabled. She hauled her considerable five-months-and-counting mass carefully to the first rung, the second. She hammered the hook home, climbed down just as carefully and picked up the print, then made her way up again. She hooked the wire, leaned back a little to check the alignment. Perfect.

She didn't have time to reach for support when her foot

slipped. Just a split second of terror before she was tumbling backwards. Then time seemed to slow, an eternity as her hands flailed wildly, grabbing at air, and a scream choked her throat.

She braced for the inevitable contact. The ladder creaked and wobbled, the hammer she'd left hanging at the top connected with her elbow in a knuckle of pain as it fell, hitting the floor with a deafening clatter.

For a stunned, terrifying moment she lay flat on her back, gulping air and finding none. Black stars crowded in on her, spiralling, dragging her towards darkness. 'No!' She was alone, she couldn't give in to the overwhelming need to close her eyes.

Gingerly she moved each limb and found them all in working order. She breathed more easily and drew in a deep, slow lungful of cold air. It smelled of paint and dust from the floor. No broken ribs, then.

Her hands curved over her belly. 'Okay,' she breathed. 'It's okay. *We're* okay. Daddy's going to hit the roof when he hears about this.' So she wouldn't tell him; she'd say Mel came by and hung the picture.

She rolled onto her side, waited a moment, then pushed up to a sitting position, wavering while the dark spots intensified, then faded. Her elbow throbbed where the hammer had hit, and now her lower back felt as if it was on fire.

She gave herself a moment before grasping the ladder and pulling herself up. Her legs felt like spaghetti but she managed to make it into the living room. A soothing cup of warm tea…

The sudden cramp clenched like a cruel fist at the base of her spine and had her gripping the door jamb. 'Oh, God.' Sweat broke out on her brow, chilling instantly in the cool air. Terror flooded through her in a black tidal wave, but she struggled to rise above it.

Sagging against the door, she cradled her baby. 'Just a twinge,' she told herself through clenched teeth.

The pain subsided as if it hadn't happened, leaving her limp and drained. She wanted to pretend it wasn't real, it wasn't happening, a nightmare—she'd wake up and Ben would hold her and tell her everything was all right.

'Ben.' Tears sprang to her eyes. 'Come home, we need you.' But he'd still be in his meeting and wasn't due back for at least two hours. She couldn't let him disappoint Zac. The boy had been over the moon when Ben had bought him his own guitar.

Another stab of pain shot up her back, lightning-hot, radiating outward, searing muscle and bone, until she gasped and doubled over. When it passed she lifted her head and saw the framed honeymoon photo on the piano.

Their marriage was built around this baby. Her dreams, her man, her life, depended on this baby.

Keeping close to the wall for support, she moved to the phone, punched in 000. Her heart cried and tears overflowed, streaking her cheeks with moisture. 'I need an ambulance right away.'

She didn't remember much about the quick trip to the hospital beyond the wail of the siren, the concerned face of the ambulance officer as he worked on her and her own numbing fear. She recited Mel's phone number to him, but in her distress she couldn't remember Ben's.

Then she was being rushed down a corridor. She was aware of fluorescent lights on the ceiling, the squeak of rubber soled shoes on linoleum, the smell of antiseptic mingling with cooked cabbage.

The pain was like a living thing, clenching her belly, tearing at her insides with unrelenting claws, ripping the tiny life within her away.

Then everything went dark.

CHAPTER THIRTEEN

'THE alfresco dining area will encourage more people off the street.' Ben and John Amos, the architect, studied the renovation plans. 'We'll—'

'Excuse me, Ben, phone call for you.' Rochelle, the perky office assistant, stood at the door. 'She says it's urgent.'

Ben straightened, annoyed at the interruption. It wasn't Carissa—Rochelle would have said. 'Did they leave a name?'

'Melanie Sawyer.'

A flicker of alarm ran through him as he reached for the phone. 'Hi, Mel. What's up?'

'Ben, it's Carrie. The ambulance just brought her in. I just came on duty and—'

'What's wrong?' His voice was suddenly hoarse, his knees weak, and someone was turning a screwdriver in his belly.

'Carrie's not doing so well…the baby—'

But he was already grabbing his jacket with his free hand. 'I'm on my way.'

Adrenaline pumped through his veins as he plunged though the hotel's ornate double doors. Sweat slicked his skin even as a chill wind swept the pavement and snuck under his shirt, sending his tie flapping over his shoulder.

To save time he hailed a cab, then cursed Sydney's traffic from the back seat as they crawled along streets crowded with cars and lunch-hour shoppers. He drummed his fingers on his knees, then clenched them around his tie before tugging it off and stuffing it in his jacket.

What the hell had happened? He'd not stopped long enough to get details. Carissa had been fine this morning, eager to sew the nursery curtains ready for him to hang.

The baby. His stomach knotted with fear and a frustrating helplessness. She was only five months pregnant—not enough time— He snapped off that train of thought and glued his eyes to the road, as if he could will the traffic to disappear.

Before the cab drew to a halt he threw a fistful of notes on the seat, muttered a terse, 'Thanks,' and was out and racing for the hospital doors. Sterile air-conditioning greeted him as he raced for the desk. 'Mrs Jamieson,' he demanded. 'Where is she?'

The receptionist looked up, frustratingly cool and business-like. 'Are you a relative?'

'I'm her *husband*.' He raked his hair. 'Where is she?'

She consulted a board. 'She's on the third floor. Ask at the nurses' station.'

He didn't wait for the elevator.

Melanie was wringing her hands when he arrived out of breath from his dash up three flights of stairs.

'Ben.' The way she looked at him, the sadness in her eyes, her hand closing over his…

His heart dropped like a stone. Dear God, he'd never known such fear. He didn't want to hear the words. The world he'd built over the last few months was about to crash around his ears and he didn't know how he was going to build it again. 'Carissa, is she…?' His voice, choked and harsh, threatened to break.

'She's still in Surgery. Ben, the baby…' Her eyes filled. 'I'm so sorry.'

Black agony twisted inside him. He beat back the pain and said, 'When can I see her?'

'I'll go check for you.'

He paced, hands shoved in his trouser pockets.

She returned a moment later. 'She's in Recovery. She'll be in room 34A when they bring her down.' She gestured and they walked down the corridor together. 'You might want to go home, grab a few things for her.'

'I'm not going anywhere until I've seen her.'

'Okay, you can wait in her room, or there's a common room with a TV, but it might be a while.'

'As long as it takes,' he said grimly. 'How did it happen?'

'You'll have to ask Carrie. She was in too much distress to talk.'

They reached the room. Melanie poured him a glass of water from a pitcher and put it on the bedside table. He shrugged off his jacket, rolled up his sleeves and sat down on the hard plastic visitor's chair.

He felt as if he were sinking into a dark abyss. *Ben, the baby moved.* The image of that day was crystal-clear. He'd known that day, known his heart was hers, but he'd been too afraid, too stubborn to acknowledge it. Now maybe it was too late.

This was to be his personal hell for what had happened in Broken Hill. His hell seemed to be watching those he cared about suffer. But Carissa? She wasn't guilty of a crime. Her big mistake was shackling herself to someone like Ben Jamieson. He had a knack for hurting everyone he cared for most. She'd be better off without him.

Melanie laid a hand on his shoulder. The gentle empathy in her touch tore another piece of his heart. 'Ben, I have to go. I don't get off till tonight. I'd stay but Emergency is short-staffed. Will you be okay?'

'Sure.'

Like hell. The moment Melanie left he was up and pacing again. His child was gone and his wife—God only knew what was happening to her. Every time a gurney came into sight his heart stopped. Every time he demanded to know what was going on he got the same evasive answer. *She's still in Recovery.*

When they wheeled her in several black coffees later, Ben was practically climbing the walls. No amount of cajoling, demanding, pleading had gotten his wife here earlier.

The first glimpse of her face, as white as the sheet, the bruised colour beneath her closed eyes, had his gut twisting into knots. 'How is she?' he asked the accompanying nurse. He hovered over Carissa while the orderlies transferred her to the bed.

'She's going to be fine.'

His heart squeezed tight as a fist in his chest. He reached for her hand, twined her limp fingers in his, willing her to open those lovely blue eyes and see him so he could talk to her, tell her she had to get well because he needed her.

'She'll sleep for a while,' the nurse said, checking Carissa's pulse. 'She might like some of her own things around her when she wakes up. Why don't you go home, pick up a pretty night-dress and some cosmetics?'

'She might like her husband here when she wakes up,' he replied tautly without taking his eyes off her. Then again...

He pressed the heel of his free hand to his brow. Would she want him now the baby no longer existed? The question shivered through him like ice-water, leaving him chilled to the bone. It wasn't a question he was ready to tackle right now.

He squeezed her hand gently, untangled her fingers from his, then lay her hand on the sheet and whispered so only she could hear. 'Carissa? I'll be back very soon.'

Carissa didn't want to wake up. She wanted to stay in that dark place where there was no pain, no loss, no heartache. Nothing. But someone seemed determined to bring her back. The layers of mind fog lifted, revealing a grey world where life no longer held any meaning.

Sterile smells of hospital sheets, disinfectant and antiseptic. Impersonal sounds—the clank of metal trolleys, the hum of air-conditioning. A stranger's hands, prodding, pressing, saying her name. She sank back to the dark.

After several attempts—over how long? She didn't know—she reluctantly opened her eyes. She noted without interest that she'd been moved to a private room.

'Hello, Carissa.' The nurse taking her blood pressure smiled, finished her task, jotted notes on her chart. 'Try to drink.' She held a glass of water with a bent straw to Carissa's lips.

Her mouth was dry and tasted like chaff, the water cool and soothing. 'Thank you.'

'Use this if you need anything,' the nurse said, pressing a buzzer into her hand.

Carissa heard the woman's footsteps recede and stared up at the cold fluorescent light. Nothing could soothe the despair that surrounded her like the dark clouds beyond the window. Every part of her body ached and the chill of the winter evening outside seemed to settle in her bones.

No one had told her, but she knew she was no longer pregnant. She clenched a hand over the place where only hours ago she'd felt it kicking. Now all she felt were contractions—angry fists of pain deep inside where her womb had betrayed her.

She remembered her ultrasound. *Look, Ben, its little heart's beating like it's run a marathon already.*

Her heart shattered. She'd never looked on her child's face, would never touch that satin-soft baby skin or hold it to her breast, would never hear its first cry or exclaim over its first smile.

She felt empty, numb and alone. She wanted the only other person who understood, who'd share her misery. Ben.

Where was he? Why hadn't he come? She watched the clouds darken and lights wink on in nearby buildings as night closed in. Their marriage was built on a mutual agreement to care for their child. That foundation was gone.

And it changed everything.

She didn't want to go back to her life without Ben. A life

without love was only half a life. Even if the person you loved didn't return that love in full measure, it was better than nothing at all. While he stayed, there was hope. She knew him well enough to know he wouldn't up and leave her until she recovered.

Or would he? If he knew what she'd done, would he turn his back on everything they'd made together? She closed her eyes. He'd been so adamant about not climbing the ladder. She'd promised. But she'd had to do it her way.

He'd trusted her to carry his baby and she'd failed him, failed herself. The bright after-pains clenching her belly were nothing compared to the emotional agony tearing at her heart.

Leave the ladder climbing to me. Had she listened? Had she waited? A cold she'd never felt before crept into her bones, and she hunched deeper into the unyielding hospital mattress with its clammy rubber under-sheet.

No, she'd had to hang that picture herself. Now she'd have to live with the consequences for the rest of her life. Not only her. Why did she think it was only about her?

She fought the drugging effects of the medication. The need to talk to Ben was stronger than her urge to simply close her eyes and drift away.

With nothing to hold him, he could be gone in a matter of weeks—or days—because when he learned what she'd done he'd leave. How could she live in that house without it reminding her of him? The king-size bed where they'd made love and plans, the horseshoe he'd nailed over the door on their wedding day, the chip in the kitchen bench-top when he'd dropped the hammer.

She'd tell him the truth. If there was to be nothing between them, at least there'd be honesty.

That now familiar warm sensation stroked her like a velvet glove, and she knew he was there before she looked. Propping up the doorway, big and sexy and male, just as he had the first time she'd seen him at the piano bar.

But this was different. They were different. Bitter-sweet pain clenched in her chest. She knew his strengths, his fears, his past, his body, just as he knew hers. It might have been enough to build a life on, a family.

'Ben…' She lifted her hand, watching, waiting for him to do something—anything. His hair was spiked with rain, his T-shirt rumpled as if he'd thrown on the first one he'd come across.

For a few seconds that stretched to eternity their gazes remained locked and a shared well of pain seemed to open up between them.

'You're awake.' His voice sounded tired and rusty as if he hadn't used it in a long time. Then he moved towards her as if the world dragged at his feet. 'I wanted to be here when you woke.' He shoved a hand through his wet hair. 'Dammit, I should've been here.'

'You're here now, that's all that matters.'

He put her overnight bag on the bed. 'Some comforts from home.' He stood, awkward and uncertain, as if he'd run at the least opportunity.

'Thanks.'

'Carissa, I…oh, God, Carissa.'

Metal creaked as he sat down heavily on the bed. Then he was clutching her shoulders, burying his head against her neck. He smelled of rain and sweat and an underlying hint of the cologne he'd used this morning.

This morning—a world away, another lifetime away. *Need any help in that shower? I'll pick up a pizza on my way home.*

His big body heaved and she knew he was crying inside. A man like Ben didn't wear his emotions for the world to see, not even for his wife. Her own tears, which she'd kept dammed, fell like a silent river for both of them.

His eyes were over-bright but dry when he lifted his head and smoothed her hair gently from her face. 'How are you doing? Sorry, stupid question.'

'I've been better.' She knuckled a damp cheek.

'Let me.' He cradled her face in his palms as if she might break and smoothed his thumbs over her cheekbones. 'You're a strong woman. You'll get through this.'

'I'm sorry, Ben, so sorry.'

'Hey,' he said softly. 'It's not your fault.'

Guilt and misery stirred a deadly cocktail with the drugs in her stomach. Her head felt like a melon, too heavy to hold up.

'Here.' He unzipped the bag and pulled out a parcel.

'A CD player. And Chopin.' She shook her head, forced a smile. 'Only you would think of that.' Only you.

'And a nightshirt. Let me help you put it on.'

He untied the hospital gown, eased it down over her shoulders. His eyes narrowed and his lips compressed when he saw the swollen purple bruise on her elbow. 'What's this?' And shoved the sheet down to her waist. A similar discoloration bloomed beneath her left breast. 'What the hell happened?'

She wanted to pull the sheet over the evidence, but the damage was done. 'I…slipped. Next thing I knew I was flat on my back.'

'Slipped? On what?' He touched her cheek. The infinite gentleness made her want to cry all over again. 'Carissa. Are you in pain? Shall I call a nurse?'

She shook her head. 'No.'

He clasped her hands in his. 'What did you slip on?'

'Slipped *off*,' she began. The need to sleep was dragging her down but she owed him the truth first. Feeling vulnerable, she tugged the sheet back up over her breasts. 'It was more like slipped off. The ladder.'

'The ladder.' Oh, his face. In that single moment she saw disbelief turn to shock. His hands slid from hers. 'You went up the ladder.' His voice was dangerously soft.

The silence rose like a living thing, broken only by the faint hum of the air-conditioning and the patter of rain on the window. A wall dropped between them. An impenetrable barrier she didn't know how to broach.

'I was only two steps up...' she said into the silence. 'I wanted to hang the picture... The hammer caught my elbow on the way down.'

She forced her heavy-lidded eyes to meet his. Grief and dark emotions she couldn't read swirled in those deep green eyes. Another tear spilled over to sting her cheek. This time he didn't attempt to wipe it away. Didn't try to touch her at all. Everything—her own grief, the guilt, the love, twisted inside her.

'Well,' he said at last. 'That'll teach you.'

She heard it all in those few words, the cold, hard finality of a door slamming shut. Her world was spinning apart and she couldn't catch the pieces fast enough.

'Put this on.' He eased her nightshirt over her head, helped slip her arms through the sleeves, but his hands might have been those of any nurse or care-giver.

He was pulling away, physically and emotionally. She wanted to wrap her arms around his neck and never let him go. 'Ben...' His name seemed to be all she was capable of. The residual anaesthetic was a dark mist enveloping her. She couldn't fight it anymore.

'You need to rest,' she heard him say as her eyelids drooped shut. But she felt callused fingers cup her jaw. 'Keep that chin up, Carissa, and you'll be okay.'

Ben breathed a sigh of relief when those eyelashes drifted closed. He waited a few moments to make sure she was asleep before pressing his lips gently to her forehead, her eyelids and finally to linger on that beautiful cushion-soft mouth before dragging himself up.

If he'd had to look at those grief-stricken baby blues a moment longer he'd have lost it right there in front of her. His control was hanging by a hair, his throat was a desert, and there was a fire in his chest that was consuming his heart, beat by agonising beat.

Their baby was dead.

He wanted to wrap his arms around her and never let her go. But now, for Carissa's sake, for her future, he had to be strong, to pull back and play the role of carer and friend. That was what she'd want. Not a lover, not a husband. Intimate sexual contact would remind her of what they'd made and lost.

So he did what Ben Jamieson did best. He walked away.

The night was wet with a blustery wind. He welcomed the cold slap of it against his face, the sting of rain against his shirt as he left the hospital grounds and hit the footpath. He had no idea where he'd left his jacket.

A few pedestrians hurried past huddled under umbrellas, tyres swished, the occasional horn blasted as the caterpillar of cars crawled homeward.

He'd never been big on promises—careless words, easily forgotten—but he did believe in his promise to Carissa.

Nothing would come before her and the baby.

He'd let her down. If she'd forgotten her promise not to climb the ladder, he blamed his own failed promise to hang the picture. She wanted everything done yesterday, was used to doing it herself—she was like him in that way. Yet he'd left the bloody ladder in the nursery instead of putting it on the verandah out of temptation, and harm's way.

If only he'd taken that moment to hang the print before he left.

If only. His gut twisted. She wouldn't want him now. Hell, she hadn't wanted to marry him in the first place. As soon as she recovered he'd step away and walk out of her life for ever.

Over the next few weeks Carissa recuperated at home. No one could have asked for a more dedicated carer than Ben. She only had to twitch and he was there.

At odd times she'd catch herself at the closed nursery door. *Can't you see it, Ben? The light'll sparkle on the sun-catcher and I'll watch rainbows on the ceiling while I sit in the rocking chair and feed her... The cradle should go here, where we can see him from the door...*

The nursery door remained closed. Though he didn't talk about it, she knew Ben was hurting as deeply as she. In the early hours she'd wake to find the bed empty and hear him pacing the verandah.

But something good came out of those midnight sessions, even if it would ultimately take him away from her. He began playing again. His music was different now—soulful, haunting, nothing she'd ever heard before. He was composing. Once when she'd slipped out to the shed where he played at night, presumably so as not to disturb her, he'd told her to go back to bed.

Shutting her out.

Then she began to notice that more and more, he was spending the days holed up in his old room that they'd converted into an office-studio, or working at the Cove. He came to bed after she was asleep and rose before she woke. The only time they seemed to come together was for the evening meal.

It was cold outside, but Carissa welcomed the refreshing feel against her cheeks a few weeks later. 'Look, Gran, your daffodils are coming up.'

New life, new beginnings.

'You're right, Gran,' she murmured. She'd never been disappointed in the thoughts she liked to think came from the other side. It was time to tuck her love for that tiny life away in a corner of her heart and look to the future.

And she was going to give it her best shot. She was going to seduce her husband with a romantic dinner, candlelight and soft music.

Ben shrugged deeper into his jacket as he stood on Sydney's Harbour Bridge watching the ferries glide across the water. The Opera House rose like white swans over a blue lake. Traffic whizzed by with the unrelenting roar of rubber on concrete.

He'd left the architect's plans he'd told Carissa he had to work on unopened on his desk. He hadn't needed to go in to the office, just as he shouldn't be here. He should be cosied up in a warm bed with his wife, not standing alone freezing to death in a hurricane wind.

He blew on his clenched fists as he imagined how he might otherwise have spent the morning. Breakfast in bed; hot coffee and hotter woman.

It was torture lying next to her and not touching her. He ached to take her in his arms and kiss away the pain he saw in her eyes, to lose himself inside her and forget what had gone before. And not only the miscarriage. He wanted to forget they'd married because she was pregnant.

In a perfect world she'd have married him because she couldn't live without him. But this wasn't a perfect world and it was obvious she could manage just fine on her own, thank you.

He loved her independence, her strength in tough times, the way she could turn a bad situation into something better. She'd turned his life around. He loved her optimism.

He loved her.

His heart constricted with a sweet pain he'd never felt for anyone before and his fingers tightened on the cold railing. Yep, time for a reality check. He was hopelessly, helplessly in love with his wife.

And a realist knew that didn't mean happy ever after; more likely it spelled disaster. Unless he did something about it.

Turning into the teeth of the wind, he checked his watch as he began the long walk back to his office. He had a late afternoon meeting. Then he was going to take her out to dinner at the fanciest restaurant he could find at short notice. *Then* he was going to tell her.

Carissa spent the afternoon pampering her body with a bubble bath. She washed her hair and left it down so it flowed around her shoulders. Knowing Ben's preference for blue, she chose a turquoise sweater of the softest cashmere—nice to touch—over black trousers, and applied just enough make-up to bring colour to her cheeks and highlight her eyes.

By six o'clock she was ready. She'd gone for the formal dining area and covered the scarred mahogany table with her best lace cloth. Jasmine rice and chicken korma curry with coconut and coriander perfumed the air. She'd made green salad and pappadams. A bottle of wine chilled in the fridge and two fat candles waited to be lit. The music was a compromise—a compilation of slow pop favourites.

At six-thirty, Ben rang. 'Hi, listen, I'm sorry, but I'm running late. I had a meeting which ran overtime.'

Her smile at hearing his voice faded a little, but she tried for a bright tone. 'Okay, when shall I expect you?'

'I'll be an hour or so. Don't cook, I'll grab something on the way home.'

'Oh, I...' Her eyes swept the intimate table setting as she moved to the kitchen, phone in hand, and switched off the oven. But she swallowed her disappointment, the feeling she'd been let down. 'See you later, then,' she said, and disconnected.

She should have told him, but all wasn't lost. First she dialled for a cab, then she rummaged in the store room and found the old picnic basket. If Mohammed wouldn't come to the mountain...

She'd give him a surprise he wouldn't forget.

CHAPTER FOURTEEN

'SURPRISE!'

Ben was already on his way out of his office, a hot date with his wife on his mind, when he heard the familiar voice in the corridor. He banked his frustration and turned to grin at the woman with a pushchair in tow.

'Jess. What are you doing in Sydney?' With no alternative, he pushed his door wider. 'Come on in.'

'I needed a break. We both needed a break with the weather we've been having in Melbourne.' She moved in for a hug, smelling of milk and crackers. 'The plane just got in. I would've left a message, but since we're staying at the Cove, I thought I'd come up and catch you if you were here.'

'And Timmy. How's it going, champ?' The sight of the kid brought a lump to his throat, but he shoved the emotion away and gave the little guy a friendly punch on the shoulder. Timmy grinned back.

'He's walking, Lord help me. I couldn't wait for the day, now I've changed my mind.'

'They grow so quick.'

'Yeah.' Her wistful sigh echoed his own sentiments.

'How are you, Jess?'

'I'm fine. Better. It gets easier with time. So…' She plunked herself in the nearest chair. 'What have you been doing with yourself since I saw you?'

'Getting married.' He hoisted one buttock on the edge of his desk.

She stared at him. 'You? Married? When?'

'Back in April. I'm sorry I didn't let you know. It was kind of sudden.'

'I can't believe it. Love 'em and leave 'em, eh?' She grinned. 'When do I get to meet this woman who snapped up Australia's most eligible man? What's her name?'

'Carissa. How about tomorrow night? Come for tea. I'd ask you tonight, but I want to prepare her. She just lost a baby.'

Her smile faded. 'Oh, God, and here I am with Timmy. I'm sorry, Ben, I know you always loved kids.'

'It happened a little sooner than I expected.' Like ten years sooner. 'Jess…can I unload on you?' He glanced around. 'Not here. Let's grab a coffee somewhere.'

Her brows lifted. 'Trouble in paradise already?'

He hesitated. 'Could be.'

'Just answer this. Does she make your skin itch?'

His lips curved at the thought. 'Like a fever.'

'Does your heart leap when you catch sight of her unexpectedly?'

'Every damn time.'

'Would you walk through fire for her?'

'If there was a point.' He picked up a paper clip from the desk and proceeded to pull it apart. 'I…it's just that we got married bec—'

But Jess raised a palm. 'Doesn't matter. Is she the last thing on your mind when you go to sleep, the first thing you think of when you wake up?'

'Yes,' he snapped, tossing the mangled clip onto the desk as the frustration and denial he'd held inside for so long unleashed itself. 'I love her, Jess. I love her so much and it's tearing me apart.'

He watched her eyes soften as women's eyes always did at the mention of the word. He'd never understood it, until now.

She shook her head. 'You haven't told her, have you?'

He blew out a long, calming breath. 'No.'

She rose and took his face in her hands. 'Oh, Ben, for God's sake. *Tell* her. A woman loves to hear it. Every day. As often as possible. No one understands better than me you never know when you might not get another chance.'

When Timmy began to squirm and fuss, she released the pushchair's harness and pulled him onto her hip. 'Why don't we go grab that coffee? You can tell me all about it.'

As the cab slowed a short distance from the Cove Carissa prepared to take her basket of goodies, including a candle, up to Ben's office. Her heart fluttered with a mixture of anticipation and panic. All she'd left behind was her filmy white nightgown, and with any luck she wouldn't be needing it.

A couple were heading out of the hotel lobby for a stroll, a toddler hoisted on the man's shoulders, but even as she watched her hand froze on the basket.

Ben.

She felt the blood drain from her face. It couldn't be… She shrank back as they walked right past the cab—she could have reached out and touched him.

The woman was tall and slim and wearing a bohemian-type flowing dress, a felt hat perched on her head. As she linked her arm in his he smiled at something she said, showing off that cocky grin Carissa hadn't seen in too long.

She didn't realise the cabbie had come to a stop. 'Here we are, lady. The Cove Hotel.'

'I've changed my mind.' She struggled to raise her voice above a whisper. 'Take me home again.'

He shrugged and turned over the meter. 'Your money.'

Tyres screeched as he pulled into the traffic. The aroma of

chicken curry mingled with the cab's smell of vinyl and stale chewing gum as she huddled back in the seat. She'd never felt so cold and there was a horrible grinding pressure building in her chest.

She was naïve enough to think their relationship had changed. *You're mine.* To Carissa, those words exchanged the night he'd come back from Melbourne had been more binding than their marriage vows.

He'd been distant since she'd come home from the hospital; coming home late, up and gone before she woke. Now she knew why. He'd tied himself to her and now he regretted it. He didn't know how to tell her, or perhaps he didn't intend to—as she'd requested. Something shattered inside her.

She let herself into the house. Her legs seemed too heavy as she walked through the dining area with its cosy table still set for two with the remaining candle and vase of early freesias perfuming the air.

She dumped the basket on the floor. To calm herself, she broke open the bubbly and poured a generous glass. Only one, she promised herself as she set it on the piano. She wanted a clear head when he got back. Despite the evidence, she wouldn't condemn him till she heard what he had to say.

He was right about one thing—a realist was rarely disappointed, but an optimist just kept coming back for more.

An hour later, she heard the crunch of gravel as the car pulled up. She closed the piano lid, picked up her glass and went to the kitchen to wait. Nerves were twisting her empty stomach into tight little knots as she sat down at the table. She wanted to hide in her bedroom, pull the quilt over her head and pretend she was asleep, but she stayed put.

She heard the front door open, shut. Heard his footsteps coming closer. Then he was there. A whiff of some expensive women's perfume floated on the air, taunting her.

'Hi. Something smells good.' He slung his jacket over a chair.

'I assume you mean the chicken curry,' she clipped. She willed her eyes to meet his. Clear, dark green, like secret pools in a dark forest. She could lose herself in those depths.

But she pulled herself from his captive gaze and focused on his jaw. No signs of lipstick, just the stubble she loved to touch. Right now she wanted to sock it. She ground her fists together under the table instead.

He gestured to the opened wine. 'You started without me.'

'I got tired of waiting.'

'I rang, but you didn't pick up. Guess you were in the shower.'

When she didn't enlighten him, he pulled out the chair opposite hers and sat down. 'Carissa, I have something to tell you. I should have told you a long time ago but I was a coward. I was going to tell you over dinner and wine but I don't want to wait…' He leaned forward.

She leaned back. Misery slid through her body with an anger that had been building over the past two hours and now threatened to explode. That anger and pride kept her chin up, her eyes dry and her voice cold when she said, 'By all means, let's hear it.'

She thought she saw disappointment and something like panic flare in his eyes, then he shoved his chair back, slid his hands round the back of his neck. 'Perhaps I'll wait, after all. You don't appear to be in the right mood.'

'How do you expect me to be, Ben?' Without thought she tossed her last mouthful of wine at him, catching him squarely in the chest.

'Hey!' Frowning, he dabbed at the stain on his shirt. 'What the…?' Then he noticed the basket. 'What's all this?'

'*All this* is the special dinner I made for us.'

'I don't get it.'

Her lips twisted around a bitter smile. 'Oh, I think you *get it* all right, but it's not with me.'

'What the hell's that supposed to mean?'

She swiped at her eyes. 'When you called to say you'd be late I packed our meal and came by the Cove.'

'So why…? Ah, I wasn't there.' Oddly, she didn't see guilt on his face, but realisation. 'I told you I rang.'

'Why? To make another excuse? I wanted it to be special. I wanted us to…' She squeezed her eyes shut to stop the tears. 'Damn you, Ben Jamieson, I *hate* you. I'll hate you till the day I die.'

The silence was thick and tense and telling. Carissa swore she heard her heart breaking.

'That's a crying shame,' he said softly, so softly she barely heard. 'Because I love you.'

'I saw you with *her* and that…that little boy… If you want a divorce…' Then his words registered. Three little words that froze her in place. She stared at him, saw the emotions burning in his eyes. Honesty. Hope. Wariness? *Love?* A drum was pounding in her chest, violins were singing in her ears. 'Say that again. Slowly.'

'I said I love you, Carissa Jamieson. And if you'd waited long enough before crucifying me, I'd have told you. The *she* is a friend from Melbourne who called in after I rang you the first time. Her name's Jess and I invited her to tea tomorrow night. And no, thank you, I don't want a divorce. Not now, not ever. You're stuck with me.'

She pressed a hand to her mouth, cursing her verbal attack while she absorbed his words. How quick she'd been to condemn despite her intention to listen first and ask questions later. 'Ben, I thought the worst of you. I didn't give you a chance to explain. I was wrong, and I'm sorry.'

'No, I was wrong. I should have told you I love you a long time ago.' He reached over and grasped her hand in his warm one. 'I wasn't there for you when you lost the baby. All I could think was you'd married me for one reason, and that reason no longer held.

'I kept my distance to give you time to decide when you were ready to go your own way. I thought that's what you wanted. I should have asked you how you felt, but I didn't want to know the answer. I was so bloody scared it'd be the one I didn't want to hear.'

'I know how you feel because I feel the same way,' she almost whispered. 'I thought you'd no longer want me when you can have any woman you want.'

He squeezed her hand. 'Any woman? I only want you. You don't know how much I wanted to take you in my arms, how many times I turned to you in the night, wanting you, needing you. Loving you.'

Happiness and new hope blossomed inside her till she wanted to dance.

Ben turned her hand over, pressed a kiss to her palm, then pushed up from the table. 'I have to get something from the studio. I want you to go sit on our bed.'

She all but floated down the passage, grabbing freesias and candles on the way. She lit the candles so that a soft radiance filled the room, then she arranged herself demurely on the edge of the bed.

Ben came in with a guitar and seated himself on the dressing-table stool.

'A Segovia,' she murmured, running her hand over the smooth wooden surface. 'It looks new.'

'It is. I wanted to do this properly. I'm not a man who uses romantic words, Carissa. Maybe that's because I never needed them till I met you, but I do know music.'

They watched each other a moment as the beautiful notes he made washed over them. Then he seemed to turn inward, caught up in the melody.

The poignant piece he'd worked on in the shed.

He didn't need romantic words. He made love to her through his music. His heart and soul flowed through his fingers, filling hers with the passion of it, the magic of it. She wanted to weep for its sheer beauty. And for the man himself.

His eyes grew dark. The flickering light softened the sharp edges of his features, turned his hair to fire. She caught the drifting fragrance of approaching spring in the freesias, the lighter scent of sun-aired linen in the sheets. She knew she'd hold this moment in her heart for ever.

He let the last chord linger on the air before setting the instrument aside.

'That's the most beautiful piece I ever heard.'

'The inspiration's right in front of me. I called it *Carissa*. I want the world to know you're mine.' He rose and took her hand, tugging her up against him. 'I want us to start over. For us this time.'

'Yes.' Her hands weren't steady as she slid them up his still-damp shirt, unfastened the first button to explore the hard-packed chest covered in thick, springy hair.

She couldn't resist. She pressed her lips there, absorbed the taste of wine over the salty taste of masculine flesh. 'I love you, Ben.' And tugged at his belt.

'Carissa, wait…'

'No more waiting. I want you. Now.' She was shocked to hear the low, earthy demand in her voice.

'Are you sure it's okay?' He dipped his head, nuzzled her neck. 'The doc said—'

'Touch me, Ben.'

He eased those competent guitar-playing fingers over her cashmere sweater, down her sides, then leisurely up and over her breasts while he watched her. His lips were a sigh away from hers, his breath warm against her cheek.

'I once said you were a fantasy. You're any red-blooded male's fantasy. Now you're mine, only mine. I love you, Mrs Jamieson.'

He closed his mouth over hers. Even slow and dreamy, she felt the banked heat in the quiet contact. But this was how it should be tonight, a gentle celebration of loving.

Outside she heard a bird's call, the shifts and creaks as the old house settled. For a heartbeat she thought she smelled Gran's scent and knew she'd always, always remember this moment.

Fantasy and reality melded as they undressed each other then slipped between the cool sheets. *He loved her.* The words sang in her head. In her heart. And for the first time they were making love in the truest sense. She let herself soar on its wings.

Later, their bodies sated and entwined, she rested her chin on his chest and looked deep into his eyes. 'I know losing the baby hurt you too. But you know what? I think we were sent a little angel on loan for a few months to bring us together.'

She saw the emotion flare as his eyes misted over. 'An angel.' His fingertip caressed her cheekbone with infinite gentleness. 'I think maybe you're right. I have two angels in my life.'

Ben found her hand and squeezed and felt the emotions wrung from him over the past few hours pour into her. 'Carissa, you gave me back something I thought I'd lost. My belief in myself. My music dried up, but it came back, different. Better. I hear it with my soul now, not my ears. It's like tuning into the cosmos.

'But more than that, you gave me hope, lent me your strength, helped me heal. Even knowing that, I couldn't or wouldn't see what was right in front of me. A chance to build a new life, a new beginning with a woman who means more to me than anything or anyone that's gone before. I can't wait to show you off to Jess tomorrow night.'

'You've never mentioned her.'

'She's Rave's widow.'

A shadow crossed his heart, but that part of his life was over; it was time to move on.

'She's the woman you went to see when you first came.'

'How did you know?'

'A woman knows these things when it comes to her man.'

'We weren't married then.' He felt a rush of satisfaction and grinned. 'You were jealous.'

'I was not.' She sighed. 'Okay, maybe a little.'

'Ha.' He looked at her and knew he was opening doors to his life that up till now he'd kept closed.

'Let's play this scene again, starting with where you tell me you love me,' she said, trailing her fingers over his face, then down, over his chest and lower. 'And we'll move on from there.'

EPILOGUE

THE usual Saturday evening crowd buzzed in the Cove Hotel's piano bar. Ben Jamieson flicked a proprietary eye over the pianist and listened to her clever fingers on the keys. And this time she wore his rings.

Kicking back in the chair, he took a large gulp of beer and watched. That slinky sapphire number begged to be taken off. He wanted her, that was nothing new—seemed as if he'd wanted her forever. As if he'd loved her forever. No reservations, no holds barred.

As Carissa launched into another bracket of classics, her eyes collided with Ben's. Instant heat flooded her body as it always did when she looked at her husband.

Fifteen minutes later, Carissa closed the piano.

'Can I buy you a drink?' The familiar liquid voice with its hint of gravel made her smile.

'Sorry, management doesn't permit employees to socialise with guests in the hotel.'

'A walk, then.'

'Very well,' she said primly. She accompanied him past the bar, and across the foyer.

'Forget the walk.' He grabbed her hand. 'Let's break some rules and get straight to the good stuff.'

'Why, Mr Jamieson, I thought you'd never ask.'

His fingers tangled with hers. 'Do you know what I was thinking about while I was watching you play?'

'Getting naked and having your wicked way with me?'

'Got it in one.'

Then right there in the foyer, in front of all the guests and including George Christos, he lowered his lips to the resident pianist's. A sultry, body-temperature-elevating minute later he kissed his way to her ear and whispered, 'So what do you want to do about it?'

'The penthouse suite. And make it quick.'

At the top floor the elevator doors whooshed open. The scent of roses filled the air as they stepped out. Red rose petals showed the way straight to the king-size bed, already turned down and waiting. A bottle of bubbly chilled in a silver bucket.

'We'll start with a celebratory drink,' Ben said, undoing shirt cuffs and nibbling on her neck at the same time. 'And then we can get down to serious business. I've got this fantasy.' He worked his way to her ear lobe. 'You, naked but for stilettos and stockings. See what you can do while I pour the wine and I'll take it from there.'

'I'll stick to water, thanks.'

He took her shoulders and held her at arm's length. 'Since when did you refuse a hundred-dollar bottle of wine?'

'Since I learned I'm six weeks pregnant.' She planted an exuberant kiss on his mouth. 'I found out today.'

His smile was slow and devastating. 'In that case… You're a miracle, you know that?' He cupped her face with his hands and the kiss he gave her was heartbreakingly tender. 'I love you, Carissa. And just for that…'

He walked her backwards to the soft leather couch and sat her down. Tugging at the picture on the wall above their heads, he opened a safe and drew out a velvet box, then sat beside her. 'I was going to give you this when the baby was born. Then when…' He trailed off, swallowed. 'It worked out after all.'

He opened the box. A tear-drop sapphire glittered darkly against the flash of diamonds.

Carissa swallowed over the lump rising up her own throat. 'You bought this on our honeymoon. I remember the string of zeros on the price tag.' The fact that he'd bought it way back then, when their relationship had been so new and fragile, brought tears to her eyes.

'Sapphires for my blue lady.'

Much later, she rolled towards him as they lay sprawled on the bed where they'd first made love. Darkness lay like a blanket, the moon spilled through the window etching his face in silver. She kissed his chin. 'Ben?'

'Hmm?' He opened one green eye.

'This has been a beautiful night. The best. But if it's all right with you, I want to go home.'

He propped himself up on one elbow, a frown creasing his brow as he laid a gentle hand on her stomach. 'You're not sick or anything, are you?'

She smiled into the darkness. 'Not yet. I want to love you in our own bed. Let's come back here every year on Valentine's Day, and make it our other anniversary.'

'Are you sure?'

'Very.'

He kissed her slowly and purposefully in the moonlight while the scent of roses lingered around them. 'Then let's go home.'

HARLEQUIN *Presents*

Harlequin Presents brings you a brand-new duet by star author
Sharon Kendrick

THE BOSS'S MISTRESS

Out of the office…and into his bed

These ruthless, powerful men are used
to having their own way in the office—
and with their mistresses they're also
boss in the bedroom!

**Don't miss any of our fantastic stories
in the July 2008 collection:**

#13 THE ITALIAN
TYCOON'S MISTRESS
by CATHY WILLIAMS

#14 RUTHLESS BOSS, HIRED WIFE
by KATE HEWITT

#15 IN THE TYCOON'S BED
by KATHRYN ROSS

#16 THE RICH MAN'S
RELUCTANT MISTRESS
by MARGARET MAYO

I ♥ HARLEQUIN Presents

BROUGHT TO YOU BY FANS OF HARLEQUIN PRESENTS.

We are its editors and authors and biggest fans—and we'd love to hear from YOU!

Subscribe today to our online blog at
www.iheartpresents.com

REQUEST YOUR FREE BOOKS!

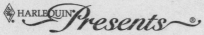

2 FREE NOVELS
PLUS 2
FREE GIFTS!

PASSION
GUARANTEED
SEDUCTION

YES! Please send me 2 FREE Harlequin Presents® novels and my 2 FREE gifts (gifts are worth about $10). After receiving them, if I don't wish to receive any more books, I can return the shipping statement marked "cancel." If I don't cancel, I will receive 6 brand-new novels every month and be billed just $4.05 per book in the U.S. or $4.74 per book in Canada, plus 25¢ shipping and handling per book and applicable taxes, if any*. That's a savings of close to 15% off the cover price! I understand that accepting the 2 free books and gifts places me under no obligation to buy anything. I can always return a shipment and cancel at any time. Even if I never buy another book, the two free books and gifts are mine to keep forever.

106 HDN ERRW 306 HDN ERRL

Name _____ (PLEASE PRINT) _____

Address _____ Apt. # _____

City _____ State/Prov. _____ Zip/Postal Code _____

Signature (if under 18, a parent or guardian must sign) _____

Mail to the Harlequin Reader Service:
IN U.S.A.: P.O. Box 1867, Buffalo, NY 14240-1867
IN CANADA: P.O. Box 609, Fort Erie, Ontario L2A 5X3

Not valid to current subscribers of Harlequin Presents books.

Want to try two free books from another line?
Call 1-800-873-8635 or visit www.morefreebooks.com.

* Terms and prices subject to change without notice. N.Y. residents add applicable sales tax. Canadian residents will be charged applicable provincial taxes and GST. This offer is limited to one order per household. All orders subject to approval. Credit or debit balances in a customer's account(s) may be offset by any other outstanding balance owed by or to the customer. Please allow 4 to 6 weeks for delivery. Offer available while quantities last.

Your Privacy: Harlequin Books is committed to protecting your privacy. Our Privacy Policy is available online at www.eHarlequin.com or upon request from the Reader Service. From time to time we make our lists of customers available to reputable third parties who may have a product or service of interest to you. If you would prefer we not share your name and address, please check here. ☐

HP08